# DUSTIN HEARD
## THE NOISE AGAIN....

In the shadows of the boxes, he thought he saw something move. Then he caught a glimpse of a pair of eyes staring at him—slitlike and blood red. He swallowed hard and was about to say something when a small gray mouse shot out from behind some papers on the floor.

Brianne laughed. "There you are. You were spooked by a mouse!"

"No, I—" he began, looking up just as the boxes came crashing down. Grabbing Brianne's arm, he managed to pull both of them to safety as boxes slammed to the floor all around them.

In the confusion he saw something leap from the top of the cupboard. It looked about the size of a cat, and it was gray.

But there was something wrong with the cat ... or whatever it was. There was something on its back ... something that looked like a pair of wings....

D0107983

**ARE YOU AFRAID OF THE DARK?**™ novels

The Tale of the Sinister Statues
The Tale of Cutter's Treasure
The Tale of the Restless House
The Tale of the Nightly Neighbors
The Tale of the Secret Mirror

Available from MINSTREL Books

NICKELODEON™

Are You Afraid of the Dark?™

# THE TALE OF THE
# SINISTER STATUES

## JOHN PEEL

A MINSTREL® BOOK

PUBLISHED BY POCKET BOOKS

New York   London   Toronto   Sydney   Tokyo   Singapore

*For the Lemon sisters—*
*June, Renee, Holli, and Felicia.*
*Thanks for the support!*

This book is a work of fiction. Names, characters, places and incidents are products of the author's imagination or are used fictitiously. Any resemblance to actual events or locales or persons, living or dead, is entirely coincidental.

A MINSTREL PAPERBACK *Original*

 A Minstrel Book published by
POCKET BOOKS, a division of Simon & Schuster Inc.
1230 Avenue of the Americas, New York, NY 10020

ISBN: 0-671-52545-X

First Minstrel Books printing March 1995

10  9  8  7  6

Cover photo by Nickelodeon/Jonathan Wenk

Printed in the U.S.A.

# Prologue: The Midnight Society

*Are you afraid of the dark?*

*I hope not. Because if you are . . .*

*Welcome to this meeting of the Midnight Society. My name is Gary, and I'm glad you've decided to join us, because I have a really interesting story to tell. It's pretty intense. In fact, I'd be willing to bet that you won't be able to move a muscle until it's finished. Just like Tim . . . but I'm getting ahead of myself.*

*Dustin is actually the hero of this story. Well, maybe "hero" is putting it a little strong. I mean. Dustin does great in school and everything—he's a straight A student—but he's not exactly hero material. He's always got his nose in a book. And his idea of a good time is to visit a museum. Now*

1

don't get me wrong ... there's nothing wrong with reading or museums. It's just that Dustin isn't the kid you'd necessarily think of calling when the going got rough.

Dustin's sister, Brianne, certainly doesn't think of him as heroic. Neither does Tim—he's one of Dustin's friends. In fact, they both think Dustin is ... well ... sort of a wimp.

But let's hope they're wrong ... very, very wrong. Because Dustin is about to face one of the most evil and diabolical forces ever to be unleashed in the modern world. And when he does, the life of his friend ... and of his sister ... will hang in the balance.

Submitted for the approval of the Midnight Society ... I call this story "The Case of the Sinister Statues."

# CHAPTER

# 1

"Get ready!" hissed Brianne Strauss, trying not to laugh out loud. She didn't want to ruin the prank she and Tim Richards had planned for her older brother, Dustin.

Tim grinned back. He raised the skeleton arm and hand he'd borrowed from the science closet. "This'll give Dustin a shock," he said softly.

Brianne slipped back into the gap between two lockers in the school corridor. She was able to see her brother as he moved slowly toward them. Tim was across the hall hidden between two other lockers. He held the arm out, ready to strike.

Dustin, as usual, was completely unaware of the world around him. He was walking and reading one of his books. If the hall had been on fire,

3

he wouldn't have noticed. Head down, he moved along, frowning as he read.

Brianne stifled another fit of giggles. Her brother really wasn't bad, but he was a little out of it. He was a straight A student, very serious, and terminally dull. He needed a little excitement in his life. He needed to be waked from his living dream. He needed a shock to make him realize there was more to life than books and museums.

As Dustin drew closer, Brianne held her breath and raised her hand as a signal to Tim to get ready. Tim nodded. All at once, Brianne brought down her hand.

Utter confusion was the result.

Tim did his part perfectly. He gave a loud, terrifying groan and lashed out with the skeleton hand. It was everything they'd hoped for and more.

Dustin leaped backward, yelped, and threw his books up in the air. Brianne and Tim fell to the floor, laughing.

But Brianne hadn't noticed the other boy in the hall. Behind Dustin was Brad Watson, the biggest bully in school. He was built like a brick wall . . . and probably, Tim said, had the IQ of a wall, too.

As Dustin's books went flying, one of them slammed into Brad's face before clattering to the floor.

4

Brianne's laughter died as she watched Brad's face turn almost purple. Dustin barely had time to realize that Brad was there before the larger boy grabbed him and spun him around.

"You little creep!" Brad snarled. "Smack me in the face, will you? Prepare to eat teeth!" He pulled back his other fist to smash Dustin.

Brianne didn't know what to do. Things were getting out of hand. But before she could panic, Mr. Bradford's voice rang out loudly. "Watson! Stop that this second!"

Brad jerked around and saw his English teacher striding down the hall toward the small group. Reluctantly Brad released Dustin, who still seemed too bewildered to realize what was happening. "Uh, we were just—" Brad started to explain.

"I know what you were *just,*" the teacher snapped. "And now you're going to *just* do detention."

With a scowl, Brad fell into step behind Mr. Bradford. As he left, he turned and glared back at Dustin. The threat was clear: this wasn't over yet.

Dustin stooped to pick up his books. "Thanks a lot," he muttered to his sister and best friend. "You've given me a heart attack and probably earned me a beating."

"We just wanted to liven up your life a bit," Tim explained guiltily.

"Terrific," said Dustin. "If you liven it up any more, I'll be dead."

Brianne scowled at him. "Well, it started *out* funny."

"Ha-ha," Dustin snapped. He'd get back at her for this. And he knew he'd have his chance the next day. Their father had to work at the university . . . and it was Dustin's job to baby-sit Brianne.

Brianne hated the word "baby-sit." She was too old to need anyone to sit for her, especially a brother who was only thirteen. And Dustin *never* wanted to do anything interesting.

But she was stuck.

And so, on Saturday morning, Dustin announced they were going to spend that afternoon at his favorite place in town—the museum.

"That place is boring!" Brianne complained. "It's filled with dust and statues and gross smells. It's Saturday, and it's spring, and I want to have fun!"

"Dad left me in charge," Dustin replied. "So I choose. And we're going to the museum."

"Can't I just kill myself instead?" Brianne begged.

"Nope," Dustin told her. "I'd be all for it, of course, but Dad wouldn't approve."

"You're all heart," Brianne growled and rolled

6

her eyes. "Can I ask Tim to come? That way, I'll have someone to talk to."

Dustin shrugged. "Okay with me."

Tim didn't want to come, but Brianne somehow convinced him. She even invited Tim to spend the night at their house. Tim's parents were away for the weekend, and Tim was staying with his older sister, who lived on the other side of town.

That was fine with Dustin. Maybe with Tim along, Brianne wouldn't spend all of her time griping about how boring the museum was.

Even Dustin had to admit that the museum wasn't the most popular place in town. As they parked their bikes at the rack in front of the building, he noticed how deserted the place was ... how very quiet.

"So," Tim asked, "which dead things are we going to look at first?"

"Not you, too." Dustin shook his head. "Don't be a pain. I've been wanting to check out the Greek room for a while, and this could be the perfect day for it."

"Yeah, right," Brianne muttered. "I've always longed to see Greek garbage."

Dustin glared at her. "You can learn a lot from the past," he told her.

Brianne was bored out of her skull after two minutes of staring at vases in the gloomy half-light. Tim yawned. "Pretty dull," he complained.

7

"I don't know what Dustin sees in this stuff. Want to go get a soda or something?"

Brianne sighed. "Dustin won't let me. I'm stuck here for the afternoon. You know, there are times when I could kill my brother. Then there are times when I know that death would be too good for him."

Reaching into his backpack, Tim pulled out a felt-tip marker. His eyes flicked around, checking out the room. No one but the two of them and Dustin way down at the other end of the exhibit room. "Well," he said, uncapping the marker, "I think these statues need a little color."

Brianne was a little shocked. "Tim, I don't know if that's a good idea."

"Relax," Tim said, pulling a tissue out of his pocket. "It'll wash off easy. No harm done. Just think of the look on your brother's face when he sees that statue over there with spots all over her." He glanced around. There was a statue of a Greek athlete with a discus in his right hand, poised and ready to throw it. "And don't you think *he'd* look great with a mustache?" Tim moved over and started to draw a handlebar mustache on the athlete's face.

He was finishing the left side when a hand shot over his shoulder and gripped his wrist.

"And what do you think you're doing?"

Brianne gasped. Tim was being firmly held by

8

one of the strangest-looking men she'd ever seen. He was tall and impossibly skinny—a skeleton in clothes, with the bare minimum of skin. She could see all the bones in his thin hands and wrists and face. His eyes glittered darkly in deep sockets. His jet-black hair looked as if it hadn't been combed in a year. His nose, the largest one she'd ever seen, was more like the beak of a parrot than the nose of a human.

"Hey!" Tim said lamely, trying to pull away. "What's your problem? This stuff will wash off in a second." But he knew he could be in big trouble. This guy, whoever he was, looked really angry.

"It's none of your business, anyway," Brianne said, jumping to Tim's defense.

"Young lady, it definitely *is* my business." The man turned his hawklike gaze onto Brianne. "I am Professor Thaddeus Stone, curator of this museum. It is my duty to look after these exhibits. This young man has vandalized one of my statues. And now"—his voice grew deep and menacing—"I'm going to call the police."

# CHAPTER 2

Brianne didn't know what to say. She couldn't deny the truth. After all, Tim was still clutching the marker he'd used. But the police! That was going too far.

"Look," she said, trying to sound reasonable. "It was just a joke. The stuff will wash off . . . really. We just wanted to get my brother—"

At that moment, Dustin finally realized something was happening, and he walked over to join them. "Uh, is there a problem?" he asked, puzzled.

"There is for this boy," Dr. Stone snapped. He gestured at the mustache. "This is his handiwork."

Dustin stared at the statue. He shook his head. "That was a dumb thing to do, Tim."

"Is that all you can say?" hissed Brianne, furious. She poked Dustin in the ribs. "Make him let Tim go."

Dustin blinked at her. "What can *I* do?" he asked.

Brianne shook her head. She should have known better than to expect help from her brother. "Look, you," she said to the man. "Can't you just let him go with a warning or something?"

Dr. Stone glared at Brianne. "Young lady, I am the head of this museum. I cannot allow people to deface these exhibits. The police will take care of this young hoodlum."

"Hey, look. It's not that big a deal. It won't happen again, I swear!" Tim begged. "If my mom finds out about this, she'll ground me for life!"

Brianne could see that Tim was really scared. He'd been dumb, and he hadn't realized how much trouble he was getting himself into.

Dr. Stone ignored him and stared at Dustin and then Brianne. Brianne felt a little chill run through her when those dark eyes fastened on hers. "And what do you think, young lady? What would be a suitable punishment for his crime?"

Brianne thought fast. "Uh . . . make him clean it up?"

"Or force him to do some work around here?" Dustin added.

Tim shot him a dirty look.

The professor's eyes narrowed. He gazed at Tim thoughtfully. Then he nodded, a satisfied smile on his lips. "All right," he said, keeping a firm grip on Tim's wrist. He looked at Dustin. "Young man, I will take your advice. You," he said to Tim, "will come with me. There is plenty of filing that needs to be done. You can spend the rest of the afternoon in my office finishing that task." He turned to Dustin and Brianne. "And as far as you two are concerned, I'll send a guard to watch your every move, so don't try anything. Perhaps this will teach you all a lesson about defacing someone else's property." He turned and began to haul Tim away.

Tim looked back at Dustin and Brianne. "See you later, guys," he said. He didn't look happy, but he had stopped struggling. The work would be no fun. But anything was better than getting the police involved. Tim's parents were really strict. If they found out about this, he'd be in a lot of trouble.

"Well, you were a big help," Brianne complained when Tim and Professor Stone had disappeared into the next room.

"Hey, I tried," Dustin answered. "Do you have a tissue?"

12

"Why?" she snapped, patting her pockets for one. "Need to blow your nose?" She handed over a mostly clean one.

"It's not my nose," Dustin informed her. He spit on the tissue and wiped the mustache off the statue. Then he wadded up the tissue and stuffed it in his pocket. "Even if Professor Stone changes his mind, Tim won't be in too much trouble with the police now," he said, smiling a little.

"Well," Brianne said grudgingly, "I guess I forgive you this time."

"Forgive me?" Dustin frowned. "For what?"

"For getting Tim into this mess," she answered. "If you hadn't insisted on coming here, he wouldn't be in trouble."

"It's his own fault for being so dumb," Dustin told her. "I'm with Professor Stone. Drawing that mustache was the wrong thing to do. Anyway, can I go back to the display cases now?"

Just then a security guard came into the room. Brianne pretended to examine a case, but she was really watching the guard watch her and her brother. The situation had been was bad enough before, when she was just bored. Now it was worse. Dustin, of course, wasn't bothered at all by the guard. That wasn't too surprising, though, since he probably hadn't even noticed him. But Brianne felt a little guilty. After all, she had been

13

with Tim when he defaced the statue. She should have tried harder to stop him.

For the next two hours the guard quietly followed Dustin and Brianne from room to room. Dustin didn't even realize they had been walking around that long. Brianne, on the other hand, checked her watch every five minutes.

They were looking at the twentieth-dynasty Egyptian artifact collection when Brianne spoke up.

"It's almost closing time," she said, pointing to an ornate old clock on the far wall. It said five-fifteen. "Let's pick up Tim and get out of here."

Dustin looked up from a display case. "Yeah. Okay," he said absently. "Let's go."

With the guard following at a discreet distance, they made their way back to the roomful of Greek statues. But Tim wasn't there.

They hung around the room for another fifteen minutes. Brianne was starting to get impatient.

"Where's Tim?" she asked Dustin.

"I don't know," Dustin answered. "Stone probably just gave him a ton of work to do. I mean, what else could have happened to him?"

The guard spoke up. "The museum is closing," he said. He took a step toward them.

"We don't need any help, thanks," Brianne said quickly. "We just want to find our friend."

"I'm sorry," the guard said. He didn't sound sorry at all. "You'll have to leave now."

Brianne shook her head. "I'm sorry, too," she said, glaring at the guard. "But we have to find our friend. Do you know where Professor Stone's office is?"

The guard looked at her coldly. Then he gestured to a hallway that led back to the Egyptian area.

"Come on," Brianne said impatiently to her brother. "Before he kicks us out." Then she headed down the hallway. Dustin followed.

As Brianne entered the main Egyptian room, she noticed a side corridor with a chain across it. A sign on the chain read Employees Only. "Stone's office must be down there," she said, looking down at the chain. Tim had already gotten into enough trouble for all three of them. She didn't want Stone yelling at her because she'd ignored some stupid sign.

But before she could figure out what to do, the professor himself appeared from another corridor down the hallway. He saw Dustin and Brianne, and nodded. Then he walked toward them.

"So," he said briskly, rubbing his hands. "Time for you two to go home, I think. Have you managed to stay out of trouble?"

"Yes, sir," Dustin spoke up. "We were just looking for our friend, Tim."

The museum curator nodded. "Your friend worked out very well," Stone admitted with a satisfied smile. "Very well indeed. So I let him off early. Didn't you see him? He left over an hour ago."

Brianne and Dustin looked at each other. "We haven't seen him, sir," said Dustin. "But I'm sure he's around here somewhere. Thank you."

Stone nodded again. Then he turned on his heel and went back down the corridor.

"What's going on?" Brianne whispered to her brother. "Why didn't Tim find us when Stone let him go?"

Dustin shrugged. "Maybe Tim headed outside. He could be waiting for us there."

But when Dustin and Brianne left the museum, there was no one in sight. And their bikes—including Tim's—were still chained to the rack in front of the building.

"You see?" Brianne said. "He didn't go anywhere. He's got to still be here."

"Yeah," Dustin said. "He's probably figuring out some other trick to pull. Well, I don't know about you, but I'm going home. Tim can come over when he's good and ready." Dustin began unlocking his bike.

Brianne just stood and stared at him. "Boy," she said. "You're something. Your best friend disappears, and you just leave."

16

"Brianne." Dustin looked at his sister. "Tim hasn't disappeared. We just don't know where he is. So cool down, okay? He'll be at our house for dinner. Trust me. Tim never misses a meal."

But Dustin was wrong. Tim still hadn't shown up when Mr. Strauss arrived home from work at seven o'clock.

"Wasn't Tim supposed to be staying over?" Mr. Strauss wanted to know as he prepared dinner.

"Yeah," Dustin said. "But we lost him at the museum. He probably went back to his sister's house."

Brianne shook her head. Why would Tim go back to his sister's? She knew he hated staying there almost as much as she hated being baby-sat by Dustin.

The three of them ate dinner. Afterward, Dustin went to his room to do some homework. Brianne went into the family room to watch TV, but she couldn't concentrate. She was still wondering about Tim. Finally she got up and went upstairs.

Dustin was lying on his bed, reading. Brianne went over and sat at his desk. "Tim wouldn't have gone to his sister's," she said, picking up a pencil. "He was supposed to stay here."

Dustin didn't even raise his eyes from his book. "Maybe he changed his mind," he said.

Brianne frowned and chewed on the eraser.

17

"Yeah. Maybe he got mad at us for not sticking up for him more," she said uncertainly.

Dustin looked up at Brianne. "I wouldn't worry," he said. "What could happen to anyone at the museum?"

Brianne shook her head. "I guess you're right. I mean, it's just a place full of dead things, like Tim said."

"Look," Dustin said. "There's an easy way to find out where Tim is. Let's call his sister."

Brianne nodded. "Okay," she said. "And when you talk to him, you can tell him you're sorry for getting him into trouble."

"Hey!" said Dustin. "*I* didn't get him in trouble . . . remember?"

But Brianne was already dialing Sandy Richards's number.

The phone rang three times before Tim's sister Sandy picked it up. Brianne could hear a baby crying in the background.

"Hi," said Brianne. "This is Brianne Strauss."

"Oh, hi, Brianne," said Sandy. "Is everything okay? I can't stay on too long—the baby's feeling cranky. Does Tim need anything? Does he want to talk to me?"

Brianne bit her lip. "Uh . . . no. Everything's fine. I was just calling to say . . . Tim will be back tomorrow afternoon."

18

"Oh, fine," Sandy said. "Well, you kids have a good time."

Brianne slowly hung up the phone. Then she turned to Dustin. "Tim's not there," she said.

"He's not?" For the first time, Dustin looked interested.

"No," said Brianne. "I didn't want to say anything to Sandy. I mean, it's probably nothing. But where could Tim be?"

"Look," Dustin said. "Tim probably just decided to sleep over somewhere else or something."

Brianne rolled her eyes. "That's lame. Why would he do that?"

"I don't know," Dustin said. "But Tim can take care of himself."

Brianne shook her head. "This whole thing is weird. Tim is supposed to be here. Maybe we should tell Dad."

Now it was time for Dustin to shake *his* head. "Tim would never forgive you," he said. "You know how strict his mom can be. She'd kill him if she found out about this."

Brianne nodded. "Yeah, I know. So what *do* we do?"

Dustin thought for a moment. "Okay," he finally said. "Let's be logical. Tim will probably call or show up tonight. But if he doesn't, we'll go back to the museum tomorrow morning. If Tim's bike is gone, at least we'll know he went somewhere else. And if it's still there . . ."

Brianne suddenly shivered. "Maybe Tim never left the museum." Brianne looked at her older brother. "What could have happened to him?"

Dustin had to admit that he hadn't the slightest idea.

# CHAPTER 3

The following morning Dustin woke up early. He rolled over in bed and frowned. Tim hadn't called. Neither had anyone else.

At breakfast, he and Brianne exchanged glances. What had happened to Tim? They ate in troubled silence.

"Maybe we *should* tell Dad," Brianne whispered as they dried the dishes.

"Tell him what—that Tim's disappeared?" Dustin shook his head. "We don't really know that for a fact. Besides, we don't want Tim to get in any more trouble than he is already. Let's go see if his bike is still in front of the museum."

When Dustin and Brianne were done cleaning up, they rode their bicycles to the museum.

Heavy rain clouds covered the sky as they ped-aled the several blocks to the museum. As usual, the building appeared to be almost deserted. The sky was a peculiar greenish color, and the air smelled like rain. Dustin managed to smile at his sister as lightning forked in the distance. "This has to be the first time you've ever come here without complaining."

"Yeah, well, for once we're looking for some-thing living," she said.

A few drops of rain fell as they reached the museum. The building loomed above them like Dracula's castle, cold and forbidding in the dark-ening gloom.

In front of the building, chained up just where he had left it, was Tim's bike.

"You see?" hissed Brianne. "I knew it! Some-thing's happened to him ... right here at the museum!"

"What could have happened to him here?" Dustin wanted to know. But he was beginning to think that maybe something *had* happened to Tim.

"Remember that guard who was watching us yesterday?" Brianne said. "He looked creepy. I mean, he didn't have to follow us so closely. I'll bet he kidnapped Tim and is holding him some-where in there for ransom. Maybe he was even going to kidnap us, and—"

22

Dustin stared at his younger sister. "Come on," he said, interrupting her. "Your imagination is running away with you. The museum guard was just doing his job. There's got to be a more reasonable explanation."

"Okay." Brianne glared at Dustin. "*You* come up with one."

"I have no idea," Dustin said. "He probably just left here without his bike and walked somewhere. But I think we should go inside and talk to Stone again. Maybe Tim said something that will give us a clue."

Dustin paid the admission fee at the front door and then asked if he could see Professor Stone. The ticket taker shrugged. "Better ask in the Greek and Egyptian galleries," she suggested. "I doubt if he's even in today."

Dustin nodded. Lightning flared and thunder cracked as more raindrops spattered the front walk outside. He'd never considered that the professor might not be at the museum. "That could be a problem," he muttered.

"Where else would the old fossil be?" Brianne whispered. "I mean, he didn't look like he had a life."

"You don't have to be mean," Dustin said, hurrying toward the Greek room. The overhead lights were turned on, and long shadows followed them along the walls. "Professor Stone hasn't done anything wrong." He stopped in the doorway to the room and glanced around, looking for a guard. There was no sign of anyone. Then he focused on something on the other side of the room. He frowned. "That's odd."

"Oh, don't start," Brianne begged as he moved farther into the room. His footsteps echoed in the gloomy space. The gallery was darker now because of the sheets of rain covering the window. "We're not here to look at stuff, remember?" she said.

Dustin ignored her and continued across the room to an empty display. "Look at this," he said. He gestured at a small sign: Removed for Study.

"Yeah, big deal," said Brianne wearily. "Now let's go," she hissed.

"You don't get it, do you?" he asked her. "That's where the statue of the Greek athlete was yesterday. The one Tim drew on and now it's gone."

Brianne shrugged. "Maybe they took it away to clean it," she suggested. "Stone was probably so upset that he ran it through a car wash or something. Who cares?"

"I just think it's odd that Tim and the statue both disappeared on the same day," Dustin said slowly.

"Right, big mystery," snapped Brianne, as a burst of thunder rocked the room. "Maybe they were both abducted by that creepy guard. Come on! We have to find Professor Stone, remember?"

Dustin gave the empty spot one last glance. "There's something very strange about this," he said.

"You're what's strange about this," Brianne replied. "Let's try the Egyptian area. Maybe we'll find Stone there."

Dustin led the way, his eyes open for a security guard. Normally, they were everywhere, but today there were none. *Just bad timing,* he told himself.

He led the way into the large Egyptian collection, one of his favorite spots in the museum. There were lots of statues, several cases of jewelry and pottery, a number of mummy cases, and two genuine mummies. There were even two embalmed cats, mostly bald, with a few stray hairs poking out of their dried-up bodies. And there was a mummified crocodile wrapped in dirty linen bands except for its head. The mouth was drawn back in a death grin, useless yellow teeth sticking up out of shriveled gums. It was a terrific collection. The only thing it lacked was someone to help them. "Great," Dustin muttered. "What do you have to do to find a guard around here?"

"Break something," Brianne suggested. When Dustin gave her a horrified look, she said, "I was *joking,* okay? I'm open to ideas."

Dustin looked around and saw a side exit with

25

an Employees Only sign. "We could try down there," he said. "That's where Professor Stone's office is." The hall was dimly lit.

"Makes sense," Brianne conceded. Lightning lit up the windows, and for a split second Brianne could see ghostly reflections of herself in all of them. Then the reflections vanished.

"Let's go," she said, shivering slightly.

Dustin ducked under the chain and peered down the short marble corridor to the end, where it turned to the left. "Stick with me."

"Trust me," Brianne said. "For once I won't leave your side. This is one place I don't want to get lost."

The corridor was lined with cardboard boxes and papers, all scattered around in messy piles. At the corner, Dustin saw that the corridor went on for forty more feet. Built-in cupboards lined one wall, with several doorways leading off it.

"The doors probably lead to offices," he suggested. "I doubt there'll be any people working today, but it's worth a shot."

"Then let's start knocking," Brianne whispered impatiently. She started off down the corridor, her sneakers squeaking. Dustin hurried after her. The first two doors were locked. Nobody answered when they knocked.

They passed a door that obviously led outside, probably to an alley. They could hear the rain pounding the pavement. There was a rusty chain across the door, which was slightly ajar. Somebody had set a box in front of it to keep it from opening farther. Dustin scowled. "That's pretty careless," he commented. "A burglar could get in here easy."

"So who'd want to rob this place?" Brianne asked. "They couldn't pay me to take this stuff away. Come on." She jumped as lightning and thunder shook the building from directly overhead.

Dustin jumped, too. "Did you hear something?" he asked.

"Apart from the worst rainstorm ever?" Brianne replied. "Our bikes—"

"Listen a minute," Dustin said. "It's inside, nearby. Kind of a scratching noise—"

"I thought it was you scratching for fleas," Brianne shot back. Then she shut up and tried to listen through the rain.

Dustin heard the noise again. It sounded as if something sharp, like a claw, was scraping on wood, but he couldn't figure out where the noise was coming from. It could have been above them. . . .

"Birds on the roof," Brianne suggested.

"There's a floor over us," Dustin pointed out.

"Maybe visitors right upstairs," she answered.

Dustin shook his head.

27

He glanced at the closest cupboard. Several boxes were piled on top of it.

Dustin stared harder. In the shadows of the boxes, he thought he saw something move. Then he caught a glimpse of a pair of eyes staring at him. They seemed to be slitlike and blood red. He swallowed hard and was about to say something when a small gray mouse shot out from behind some papers on the floor.

Brianne laughed. "There you are," she said. "You were spooked by a mouse."

"No, I—" he began, but was interrupted by a noise from the top of the cupboard. He looked up just as the boxes came crashing down. Grabbing Brianne's arm, he managed to pull both of them to safety as boxes slammed to the floor all around them.

In the confusion he thought he saw something leap from the top of the cupboard. It looked about the size of a cat, and it was gray.

But there was something wrong with the cat . . . or whatever it was. There was something on its back . . . something that looked like a pair of wings. . . .

# CHAPTER 4

By the time Dustin looked down the corridor, there was no sign of either the mouse or the other thing, whatever it was. Shaken, he turned to his sister. "Did you see that?" he asked.

"Just some dumb cat chasing a mouse."

Dustin wondered if he should say anything about the wings.

No, Brianne wouldn't believe him. In fact, he wasn't sure he'd seen anything odd himself. Maybe it *was* just a cat.

Just then a door farther down the hall popped open, and Professor Stone thrust his skull-like head out, his mop of black hair bouncing. When he saw Dustin and Brianne, he came out into the hall. "What are you doing here? This area is off limits to all but museum staff. You must leave this minute."

Dustin forced himself to stand still. "Uh, actually, we wanted to see you, s-sir," he stammered as the lights flickered.

"Well, I don't want to see you," Stone growled, wrinkling his nose. "I'm extremely busy with some important research. And I had better not see you in ten seconds, or one of the guards will throw you out!"

Brianne spoke up. "We just want to know what happened to our friend Tim Richards," she said. "You were the last person to see him, and now he's missing."

Stone turned to her. "I have no idea what you're talking about."

"Tim is the boy you were going to have arrested yesterday," Dustin explained. "When he drew the mustache on the statue?"

"Oh, him." Stone raised his eyes to the ceiling. "He was here for an hour or two. After that, I don't know what happened to him. Furthermore, I don't care."

"But we have only your word that you let him go," Brianne said defiantly.

Stone looked down at the girl, his eyes narrowing. "I assure you I didn't keep him with me any longer than necessary."

"What about that guard?" Brianne went on. "Can we talk to him?"

Stone looked startled. "The guard? What guard?"

"The one who was watching us yesterday," Dustin said.

Strangely, Stone seemed relieved. "Hopkins? It's his day off. And I assure you ... he hasn't seen your friend, either."

"How do you know?" Brianne asked.

"Because I do!" Stone said. He looked angrily at Brianne. "You are interrupting important work," he went on. "I have no time for this foolishness. Wherever your friend has gone, he's better off there, I assure you." He raised his voice. "Guard! Guard!"

"Oh, great," muttered Brianne. "Now we get tossed out in the rain."

At that moment a security guard swaggered out of Stone's office. He moved around Stone and came slowly toward Brianne and Dustin. "Shall I remove them, sir?" he asked. He spoke with a foreign accent.

"We're cool," Brianne said, forcing herself to smile. "We were just leaving. Honest." Grabbing Dustin's arm, she half-led, half-dragged him away. "Let's get out of here," she muttered. "That guy's built like a wrestler."

The guard moved toward them. Brianne and Dustin walked quickly away. The guard followed.

"What does he want?" Brianne hissed.

Dustin turned to the guard. "We're fine now. You don't need to follow us through the whole museum...." Dustin's voice trailed off.

The guard's uniform was pulled tight across his chest and arm muscles. His gaze was cold and forbidding. Under his peaked cap he had thick, curly black hair and a very familiar face.

Where had Dustin seen that face before?

"Come *on*, brother dear," said Brianne, grabbing Dustin's jacket. They turned and walked quickly back the way they had come.

They had just reached the Greek room where the missing statue had been when Dustin stopped short.

The guard's face! Now he remembered where he had seen it before....

But it wasn't possible!

# CHAPTER 5

"Did you see that guard's face?" Dustin asked weakly as Brianne led him toward the exit.

"Of course," Brianne replied. "That's why I knew it was time to get out of there."

"No, I mean did you really *see* him?" Dustin was shaking. "The statue of that Greek athlete Tim drew a mustache on—remember? The one that's missing? Well, the guard was a dead ringer for that statue!"

Brianne shrugged. "So? He may have looked a bit like the statue."

"Not a bit," Dustin argued. "Exactly."

They were back in the lobby now. Brianne glanced around, but no one was following them.

"What do you mean?" she asked, puzzled. She sat down on a bench.

"I don't know," Dustin admitted. "Except I don't think that guy just *looked* like the statue."

Brianne didn't know what to say. She just stared at her brother. Finally she shook her head and spoke. "What's your point?"

Dustin felt his face burn as he squirmed. "I don't know. Look. I'm usually the logical one here. But I have a feeling about that guard. I mean, he really looked like that missing statue. It's like . . . the statue came to life or something. I know it sounds a bit bizarre—"

"A *bit?*" Brianne snorted. "That's like saying the Empire State Building is a *bit* tall."

"I don't care what you think," Dustin replied. "That guard looks *exactly* like the statue."

Brianne sighed theatrically. "So you think that guy is a statue? You've been reading too many science fiction books. Why don't you watch TV like a regular human being?"

"I'm not saying he *was* the statue," Dustin said. "And I know it sounds weird. But what if . . . I don't know. What if somebody was making fake statues, and they used that guy as a model, and they were selling the real ones? The stuff in this museum is worth a fortune."

Brianne sighed again. "Look, just forget that I'm your kid sister and try to think of me as an average person. If any average person heard you say that someone had taken that statue off its pedestal—"

"Plinth," Dustin corrected her automatically.

"Whatever." Brianne rolled her eyes. "Anyway, if you're saying that someone took a ten-ton statue and replaced it with a gigantic fake statue and then got the real one out of here without anybody noticing—especially the paranoid professor—don't you think any average person would think you're crazy?"

Dustin blushed again. "Okay, you're right. Forget I said anything," he replied. "Forget that Tim is missing. Forget the guard. Go off and be rational about this."

"Don't get mad," Brianne told him. "I haven't forgotten anything . . . especially Tim. I just don't see how a guard who looks a little like a statue could have anything to do with our friend."

She had him there. "I don't either, really," Dustin admitted. He glanced around the empty room. "I'm just going to take one more quick look around for any clue to where Tim might be."

Brianne shrugged. "And I suppose you want me to help?"

"Unless you've got a better idea."

"None that will find Tim. Okay, I'll help." She

35

held up a hand in warning. "But that doesn't mean I accept your stupid ideas."

"Fair enough," Dustin pointed. "Let's start in the Egyptian room." He didn't know what he was looking for, but hoped he'd recognize it when he saw it. The Egyptian collection was the one he knew best. It seemed to be a logical place to start . . . if there was any logic to this at all.

The room looked the same as it had the day before. The same cases, the same sculptures. The most impressive one was a statue of Anubis, the jackal-headed god of the dead, guardian of the afterlife, and judge of good and evil. Dustin had always liked this statue. It was in great shape even though it was three thousand years old.

He tore his eyes away from the statue when he heard Brianne calling him. "What's wrong?" he asked.

"This is," she said, shaking her head in amazement. "Just look at this cat statue. It's obviously a fake!"

Dustin bent to examine the piece. It was very unusual. It wasn't just sitting there like most Egyptian cat sculptures. This cat was rearing up, ready to strike out at something. Its claws were extended and its mouth was open. He didn't recall seeing it before. The label on the base read Egyptian, Fifteenth Dynasty. "So?" he asked. "The

36

Egyptians worshiped cats. The style is unusual, but why do you think it's a fake?''

Brianne rolled her eyes. "I could have guessed you wouldn't see it." She pointed at the cat's neck. "It's wearing a flea collar, dumbo. I don't think the Egyptians had those."

"It's probably just a normal collar," he grumbled, but he bent down for a closer look. He had to admit Brianne was right. It was a perfect copy of a modern flea collar. "That's strange," he said slowly.

"It's really stupid," Brianne said. "How could this museum fall for such an obvious fake?"

"It's not just that." Dustin shook his head. "Why would anyone who was going to all the trouble of faking a copy of an ancient Egyptian statue make such a dumb mistake?"

"As a joke?" Brianne suggested.

"The faker would have to spend a lot of time making the statue," Dustin pointed out. "Why ruin it by doing something so stupid? It's just so weird," he muttered. "I think this might be a clue of some sort. The missing statue, the guard, and now this."

Brianne's eyes suddenly lit up. "What if someone was practicing making statues, and started with this cat? And maybe stole the original?"

Dustin looked at his sister. "You might be

right," he said. "But I thought you said my idea about someone stealing statues was crazy."

"Stealing giant statues *is* crazy," Brianne replied. "But stealing a cat statue . . . well, maybe that's possible." Brianne frowned. "What if Tim somehow found out and somebody kidnapped him to shut him up? I mean, if this stuff is worth that much money . . ."

Dustin nodded. "Maybe." He hesitated, staring at the cat. "And there's something else. Professor Stone must have put this statue on exhibit. Why didn't he spot the collar instantly?"

"Maybe he's not really a professor?" suggested Brianne.

"I don't see how he couldn't be," Dustin answered. "But he'd have to be a really lousy scholar not to have spotted this collar."

"Do you think he's involved somehow?" Brianne said. She frowned at the cat.

"I don't know," Dustin admitted. "The whole thing seems crazy. But you've definitely spotted something peculiar. I just wish I knew what it meant."

"Maybe I should keep looking?" Brianne suggested. She was pleased by his praise. "I can try to spot something else."

"Okay." Dustin let her go her own way. He stood in front of the cat statue, staring into space, trying to figure out how all of the clues fit together.

Maybe someone *was* making fake sculptures and stealing the real ones. But it had to be someone with real talent, someone who knew what he was doing. Why would anyone that smart carve a cat so lifelike and then ruin it with such a dumb detail? And why hadn't Professor Stone noticed the collar?

Dustin reviewed the clues: Tim was missing; there was a guard who looked just like a Greek statue, and that statue was missing; now there was a fake Egyptian cat statue.

Wait a minute. Stone had punished Tim because he'd marked up a statue—the one that the guard looked like. The whole thing might be tied in with Professor Stone. But how?

Lost in thought, Dustin turned to walk away and almost collided with somebody else who had just entered the room. He started to apologize when he realized who it was. His face fell, and he groaned. "Brad Watson!"

"Hey, if it isn't the human weenie," Brad replied with a sneer. "Just the punching bag I need to get some laughs out of this place."

Dustin could hardly believe his bad luck. "Uh, hi," he said weakly. "I didn't know you liked the museum."

"I don't," Brad said. "But I had to come for

school. This is luck. Remember I said I'd get you? Well, there's just the two of us here now."

Brad was dead right. They were alone in the Egyptian gallery. Brianne must have moved to the next room. Dustin was in real trouble.

"I hope you like the taste of blood," Brad said, grinning nastily. He pulled back his fist.

# CHAPTER 6

Dustin could think of only one thing to do. As Brad's fist shot forward, Dustin collapsed and fell to the floor. Brad was jerked forward by the force of his own swing. He stumbled heavily over Dustin and took a header . . . right into an exhibit case.

Luckily the glass didn't break. But Dustin heard the whole case rattle and Brad howl in anger and pain. Dustin knew he was going to pay for every little pain Brad suffered. Dustin jumped to his feet, aiming to take off.

"I'm gonna kill you!" yelled Brad, wincing and groaning as he staggered in circles. As Dustin started to run, Brad swung out his foot and kicked Dustin hard.

With a yell of pain, Dustin collapsed again. The pain in his ankle was bad, but he knew that worse was coming. Brad would see to that.

"Hey!" Brianne called out, from the doorway. She must have heard the noise. "What do you think you're doing, Brad Watson?"

"Making you an only child," Brad growled, grabbing for Dustin. "What does it look like?" His fist closed around Dustin's sore ankle. Dustin winced.

"Let him go, you jerk," Brianne growled.

"Aren't you tough?" Brad said. "If you feel left out, I'll save a few punches for you."

"You leave her alone!" Dustin yelled.

Brad merely grinned and twisted the ankle he held. Dustin yelped in pain, which made Brad's grin spread. "Ah, music to my ears. Sing some more, super-wimp!"

*"Enough!"*

Dustin didn't need to turn his head to know who had spoken—the voice was unmistakable. Professor Stone had shown up . . . and just in the nick of time.

The museum curator strode into the room, his dark eyes blazing. "What are you doing?"

Brad smirked. "Practicing a little dance," he said. "My partner forgot his dress, though."

Stone bared his teeth and glared at the bully. "Think you're a wit, huh?" he growled. "Well,

42

you're only half right, because you're a half-wit."
He glowered. "Your childish antics could damage
my exhibits, and I cannot tolerate that. Stop your
foolishness and get out of here now."

Brad wasn't ready to stop yet, but he did release Dustin's ankle. Wincing, Dustin managed to
stand. Brianne joined him and gave him a slight
smile.

"Look," Brad said to the professor. "You stay
out of this. It's none of your business."

"When you threaten my exhibits, it *is* my business," Stone fired back. "Leave this museum this
instant, or I shall eject you!"

"I'd like to see you try," Brad replied.

Stone was furious. "That does it!" he snapped.
"I will not tolerate such disrespect from anyone.
You will come with me this minute and be
punished."

Brad laughed, shaking his head. "You gonna
make me?" he asked. "You and what army?"

*"This* army," said a fresh voice from the
doorway.

Dustin glanced around, though he knew from
the accent who was there. It was the guard who
looked like the Greek statue. His eyes were fixed
on Brad's, and he stepped forward. "You will do
exactly as the professor instructs, or I shall be
forced to hurt you." He held up one fist, which
was the size of a dinner plate.

Brad wasn't stupid. If he started trouble, this guard was obviously prepared to finish it—fast. Brad raised his hands, palms open. "Uh, look guys, it was just a joke, okay? I'm leaving right now, right?"

"Wrong," snapped Stone. "You've gone too far. You're going to have to be punished." He gestured to the guard. "Take him away, Pericles."

"Hey, no! Wait!" Brad yelped, backing away. "There's no need for this, honest. I'll apologize, if that's what you want."

"You had your chance," Stone informed him coldly. "Now you have to pay. There's something that needs to be done ... and you are going to do it." Stone nodded to Pericles, and the powerful guard grabbed Brad by the shoulders.

Dustin didn't know what to do or say. Brad squirmed in the guard's grip and punched helplessly with his fists. Some of his blows hit the guard, who didn't seem to notice as he began to carry Brad off.

Suddenly Brad began to blubber. "Please," he cried. "Just let me go! I'll be good ... I promise!" As Brad screamed and begged for mercy, Dustin watched him, open-mouthed. Dustin was stunned— Brad Watson was a coward!

When the guard had dragged Brad off, Professor Stone turned to Dustin and Brianne, his eyes narrowed.

44

"This is the second time you two have been involved in a disturbance here at the museum," he said. "I'm beginning to dislike both of you."

"The feeling's mutual," Brianne snapped back.

"Leave the museum immediately," the professor told her. "And never come back. If you're involved in a third incident here, you will not be let off lightly. Do you understand?"

"Don't worry," Brianne replied, furious too. "You couldn't pay me to come back here."

Dustin couldn't believe it. "You're banning us from the museum?" he asked, shaken. "You can't do that! I come here all the time!"

"I *am* banishing you." Professor Stone snapped his fingers. Another guard appeared in the doorway.

"And we couldn't find one guard when we needed one," Brianne muttered.

Stone gestured at Dustin and his sister. "Escort these two to the door," he ordered. "And make certain they don't come back. If they cause you any problems, use force to evict them."

The guard nodded and glared down at Dustin and Brianne. "You going to come quietly?" he asked. He cracked his knuckles, obviously wanting them to try something.

"We're out of here," Brianne told him, throwing her head back. "Who needs your boring old museum anyway?"

Dustin sighed and fell into step beside his sister. They walked down the long, empty corridor toward the entrance, the guard behind them. It was as if they were being marched to their execution. Dustin didn't know what to do. Now how would they find Tim?

As Dustin thought about his friend, he looked up. Then he stopped dead in his tracks. All the blood drained from his face as he looked at the new statue in the entrance hall. It was of a young boy, his head thrown back, screaming. It hadn't been there earlier. On the plinth was a sign—Boy Transformed.

Dustin would have recognized that face anywhere.

"Move it," the guard snarled, giving Dustin a shove in the back that made him stumble.

"No, wait!" Dustin yelled.

"Move it," the guard repeated. "Or I'll move it for you."

Dustin was torn. He desperately wanted to go back to examine the statue. But the guard would throw him out bodily if he did. He made a quick decision and dashed after Brianne, who was already outside the main entrance and going down the steps. She turned and stuck her tongue out at the guard. "That's what I think of your crummy museum!" she yelled. Turning to Dustin, she grinned slightly. "Now I feel better."

46

"Well, I don't," Dustin answered.

The rain had stopped, but the grass was still wet. They headed for a small gazebo on the front lawn close to where their bikes were parked. Inside they collapsed onto a dry bench.

Dustin stared at Tim's bike, trying not to believe what he had seen. "That statue..." he began weakly.

"What statue?" Brianne asked. "There were hundreds of them."

"By the entrance," he said. "The one of the boy screaming."

Brianne shrugged. "I wasn't really looking at it. Why?"

"It looked exactly like Tim," Dustin replied.

His sister stared at him and then put a hand to his forehead. "You don't have a fever," she announced. "So I guess you've just cracked up."

"I have not!" Dustin said angrily. "I'm telling you, there's a new statue in there—and it's Tim!"

# CHAPTER 7

Brianne was worried. "Dustin," she said gently. "I know I tease you a lot, but that's because you're my brother. It's my job. Really, you're not too bad. But I'm seriously worried about you. I'm usually the one with the crazy imagination. You don't really *believe* these things you're saying, do you? I mean, it's impossible. No one could have made a statue of Tim overnight and then put it up in the museum. It's life-sized, right? It would take days to make. . . . Oh, it's just too crazy."

Miserably, Dustin shrugged. "I know," he confessed. "I'm not exactly a believer in weird stuff. I don't believe in ghosts or flying saucers or that Elvis is still alive. I believe in what I can touch and prove. I believe in science." Then he shook his head. "I also believe that 'coincidence' is a rotten word to explain things we don't understand. And there are too many coincidences piling up around here."

Brianne was about to say something, but Dustin raised his hand. "Let me talk this through, just once. Listen to me, and then you can argue all you want."

"Tim defaced the statue of the Greek athlete yesterday. He was caught by Stone. Tim never went home, and the statue is gone. Stone says he let Tim go, but we have no proof of that. Now, if Stone *did* let Tim go, that means something happened to Tim *after* he left the museum. That's not impossible, of course, but it is unlikely, since his bike is still here. Besides, we probably would have heard something by now.

"Today we see a new guard in the museum who looks exactly like the missing statue. Maybe that's a coincidence, but I heard Stone call him Pericles, which is a Greek name. Then we see a statue of a cat that's supposed to be Egyptian, but it's wearing a flea collar, so it's either a very obvious fake—or something else. Finally I see a statue that looks exactly like Tim—who's still missing. Okay, now each of those facts doesn't mean much alone. But when they're added to-

49

gether, something really strange seems to be going on.

"Somebody is making statues. We know that because of the cat. Maybe someone made a statue of the guard, too. Maybe not. And then there's Tim . . ."

Dustin paused for a moment. He shook his head. What he was about to say was so unbelievable that he almost didn't go on.

"I saw a film once where a mad artist killed people and then covered them with plaster so they'd look like statues," Dustin finally whispered. "Maybe that's what happened to the cat . . . and to Tim."

Brianne stared at Dustin for a long time. Then she raised an eyebrow. "My turn now?" When he nodded, she shook her head. "That's a load of garbage. You're suggesting that somebody killed Tim and hid his body inside a statue? No way. Why would anyone want to do that? I mean, what's the point?"

"Maybe," Dustin said, "it's some sort of punishment for what Tim did yesterday. All I know is, it fits the facts."

"It fits what *you* say are the facts!" exclaimed Brianne. "Okay, maybe the guard looks like the missing statue. Maybe that cat statue is a fake. Maybe the statue of the kid looks like Tim. But jumping to the conclusion that someone in the museum is a killer is a bit extreme, right?"

"Yeah," agreed Dustin. "But we do have a way to find out more."

Brianne squinted at him suspiciously. "What do you mean?"

Dustin gestured at the museum. "Stone took Brad Watson off somewhere, didn't he? In exactly the same way and for the same reason. Maybe whatever happened to Tim will happen to Brad, too."

Brianne was getting more and more worried about her older brother. "And what do you plan to do about it?" she asked anxiously.

"Today the museum closes early," Dustin explained. "It'll be closed in a couple of hours, but we can stay here and watch the place. If Brad comes out before then, I'll feel a lot better about what might have happened to Tim in there. But if he doesn't ..."

"We'll know someone in there is up to something." Brianne finished Dustin's thought for him. She thought about this for a minute. Then she shook her head. "You want me to hang around here for another two hours to check out your psycho theory?" she said weakly. "You must be joking."

Dustin shrugged. "You can leave if that's how you feel," he told her, "but Tim's my friend and

51

I'm going to stay and watch." He sighed. "Look, maybe my idea is crazy, but I've got to *know*."

Brianne studied him for a moment, and then grinned. "Well, that proves we're related," she said. "You're just as stubborn as I am. Okay, I'll wait with you. But if you're wrong and Brad comes out, I'm going to get you for this. That's a promise."

"Deal," Dustin agreed. He wasn't sure he was right, and he knew how wild his idea sounded. Actually he didn't like it much himself. But he couldn't see any other explanation.

"By the way," Brianne said, "thanks for standing up to Brad for me," she said. "I didn't know you had it in you."

"It didn't do much good," Dustin said sadly. "Brad would have wiped the floor with me."

"At least you tried." She grinned. "You're not so bad, I guess. But don't go getting the idea that I *like* you. You're still my older brother, and that makes us enemies."

"Of course," Dustin agreed. But he smiled at her just the same. Actually, he and Brianne were getting along a lot better than they ever had. Before, they never seemed to have anything in common. Now they did.

*Although I wish it wasn't Tim's disappearance,* Dustin thought miserably.

52

The next two hours felt like forever. It was bad enough watching and waiting, but Dustin was also full of doubts. Was Brianne right? Was he a fool? More than once he wanted to call off the whole thing and go home.

But he couldn't. What about Tim? And if Dustin was right, Brad was in danger too! Dustin had absolutely no good feelings for Brad, but he couldn't just leave him there in the museum when there might be a madman on the loose. Okay, he'd look like an idiot if he was wrong. But what if he was right?

Besides, there was nothing else he could do. He could report Tim missing . . . but the police wouldn't believe his theory, either. And by the time they got around to checking the museum, it might be too late.

If he was wrong, Brianne would think he was a complete jerk. And she wouldn't let him forget it in a hurry.

But, no! He *wasn't* wrong. Maybe his reasoning wasn't perfect, but that didn't make it wrong. He knew there was something going on in the museum. Maybe it wasn't exactly as he'd described it, but something had happened to Tim in that building. He could feel it in his bones.

The gazebo was under a large old oak. From time to time as they waited, Dustin could hear rustling in the branches above. Squirrels or birds, probably ... there were plenty of both.

Then Dustin heard a voice. It was nasal and deep, but fairly quiet. And it was definitely coming from above them.

"Here, you dumb squirrel," the voice whispered. "Come to Grimalkin. Over here, you jerk!"

Dustin almost jumped out of his skin. "Did you hear that?" he asked Brianne.

Brianne's eyes opened wide, and she clutched Dustin's hand. "Is someone in the tree?" she whispered.

"We've been sitting here for an hour and a half," Dustin objected. "Nobody else has come near us. Besides, who would sit in a tree for that long just to catch a squirrel?" He poked his head out of the gazebo. Then he squinted up through the branches. The sun was now low in the sky, and the light dazzled his eyes. It was impossible to see more than shadowy shapes.

"Jeez," complained the same weird voice. "What does a guy have to do to get a meal? I'm starving, and you're dancing around? When I catch you, you stupid squirrel, I'm going to bite your dumb head off!"

There was an explosion of movement in the branches. Chittering wildly, obviously terrified, a squirrel slammed through the leaves and then shot down the trunk. Squealing, it hurtled past Dustin and Brianne.

Whatever had been hunting it screamed in rage. Half a branch fell out of the tree. Dustin yanked his head back inside the gazebo. What was going on above them?

He knew he had to climb the tree to find out.

# CHAPTER
# 8

"Don't be crazy!" Brianne hissed as Dustin prepared to pull himself up to the first branch. "It could be dangerous!"

"Don't worry," Dustin said. He was worried himself, but he had to find out what was lurking above their heads.

"Why should I worry about *you*?" Brianne muttered nervously. "After all, if you disappear, I get your CD collection." But her eyes followed Dustin with genuine concern. He was proving himself a lot braver than Brianne had thought he was. She couldn't help admiring him ... a little.

As Dustin boosted himself up to the first branch, he heard a wild rustling above him. He peered up into the glistening leaves and could vaguely make out a face staring down at him. It was impossible to be positive, but the face didn't look human. It was too small, and it seemed to have a snout.

"Uh-oh," said the face. More rustling in the branches. The thing was moving higher. Where was it going? Dustin spotted a half-open window in the museum about ten feet from the tree. Could this thing be heading there?

Squinting against the sun, he saw something hurtle out of the tree and in through the window. The thing wasn't more than a couple of feet tall. And Dustin definitely saw two wings as the creature soared to the window.

Dustin scrambled back down the tree.

"Did you see that?" he asked Brianne when he reached the ground. "It flew into a window up there."

"Some kind of a bird," she said. "Somebody's pet, I guess."

"But it was talking," he objected.

"Lots of birds talk," Brianne said nervously. "Like a parrot. Stop trying to spook me, will you?" But she clearly wasn't sure what it had been, either.

Dustin could have sworn that it was no bird. It had used words intelligently. But he had no idea what the thing was or if it had anything to do with the museum.

Still, everything pointed to something strange going on in there.

Tim had disappeared inside the museum. Dustin was sure of that. And Brad hadn't come out yet, either. Dustin scanned the massive front doors anxiously. Even though he disliked Brad, Dustin couldn't let some maniac kill him.

After the last couple of visitors hurried out, the main doors were locked. Dustin gave Brianne a sideways glance.

"It doesn't prove anything yet," she objected. "The staff members are still in there. Let's wait to see if Brad leaves before they do."

"Okay," Dustin agreed. But he was more and more convinced he'd been right.

One by one the various staff members left the museum and headed home. Dustin recognized the cashier and a couple of the guards. Ten minutes after the last person left, Dustin stood up.

"I don't think anyone else is coming out," he said. "Stone and that Greek guard are still in there. And so is Brad. *Now* what do you say?"

Brianne had to agree. "It looks like you may have something. So what do we do? Call the police?"

"And say what?" asked Dustin. "By the time the police arrive, anything could have happened. And we can't tell them what I suspect. If *you* don't believe me, you can bet *they* won't."

58

"You're right about that," his sister agreed. "So what can we do?"

Dustin swallowed. "We have to go inside the museum and find proof. There are phones in there, so we can call for help if we need it. But we have to have solid evidence before we get the police involved."

"Go inside?" repeated Brianne. "Are you crazy? Do you know what you're talking about here?"

"Yes," Dustin answered slowly. "We have to break into the museum. It's the only way."

# CHAPTER 9

Brianne didn't know what to say for a moment, but then she found her voice. "Reality-check time again," she said grimly. "Breaking and entering is illegal."

"Yeah, I know," admitted Dustin. "But there really isn't any other way to get what we need. Besides, do you think what's going on in there is legal?"

"Well, no," agreed Brianne. "But what if we set off an alarm?"

"Stone's still in there, so the alarm can't be set yet."

"You know you're talking about doing something that could get us sent to a juvenile hall," Brianne argued.

"I know." Dustin stared at his sister. "It also may be the only thing that can save Brad or Tim. Are you going to chicken out on me?"

"Nobody calls me a chicken," Brianne growled, trying to hide her own fear. "And how come you're being so brave right now? You're usually the first to chicken out of everything."

"I don't know why," Dustin had to admit. "I'm just doing what I have to. I'd feel better if you came with me, but if you don't, I'm going in anyway." He started to walk around back.

Falling into step beside him, Brianne grinned. "Somebody's got to look after you, I guess, and I'm the only one around." They were entering the alley that ran along the back of the building. "But how are we going to get in?"

"When we were in the corridor that led to Stone's office, remember that door we saw—the one that was left open?" Dustin said. "It's down here somewhere. Maybe someone forgot to lock it. Anyway, we can't go in the front door. This is our only chance of getting back inside."

Brianne seemed impressed. "My brother the burglar," she said, "Wow. You'll be cutting school next."

"In your dreams," Dustin replied, smiling slightly.

They walked up the short flight of stairs to the door. Dustin glanced around. Nobody in sight.

61

The door looked as if it was locked. But Dustin turned the knob and put his shoulder to it. He managed to nudge it open several inches before it stopped. It wouldn't move any farther. He glanced down and saw the rusty safety chain in place. "Oh, great," he muttered. "That's blown it."

Brianne grinned. "Nah," she said. "It just slows us down a little." From her pocket she pulled out her Swiss army knife. "Let the pro do this bit." She stuck a blade into a link of the chain and twisted. The link gave slightly, but not enough. "I hope you're stronger than you look, 'cause I can't do this." She handed the knife to Dustin.

He took it from her and twisted as hard as he could. The rusty link snapped, and the chain rattled as it fell apart. "Nothing to it." He handed her back her knife. "Do you always carry that around?"

"You'd be surprised how useful it is," Brianne informed him. "All the best gadgets are for dismantling other people's bikes if the owners annoy you."

Shaking his head in amazement, Dustin pushed on the door again. There was a scuffling sound from inside as the door dislodged the box that was jammed against it. The door opened another foot, and they slipped inside.

There was no sign of Stone or the guard. Dustin

62

whispered, "We'd better close the door again. A guard might be patrolling or something."

"Good thinking," Brianne agreed. She moved the box back into place to hold the door. Then she picked up the broken link and used it to join the chain together again. If nobody looked too closely, it would pass. With luck, they wouldn't be discovered.

"So," Brianne asked in a whisper, "where do we start?"

"Let's check the galleries first," Dustin said. "They should be empty. Stone's probably in his office."

He started off down the marble corridor to the main Egyptian room. It was very quiet, except for the squeak of Brianne's sneakers and other slight creakings. All old buildings made noises like this, he knew, but it sounded a little like someone was groaning deep inside the museum's walls.

When they reached the Egyptian room, which was dead silent, they could make out only shadows and shapes. There seemed to be nobody there.

Even Dustin, who normally loved the museum, had to admit that it was pretty spooky. They passed into the Greek room, where it was so dark that it was impossible to tell if there were living things among the statues and relics. Dustin fought down his fears. There was probably enough real terror in this place. He didn't need to start imagining shadows shifting and moving around him.

Unless, of course, something *was* moving.

"Don't bump into anything," he cautioned his sister.

"What kind of idiot do you think I am?" she asked. "You watch yourself. You're the klutz, not me."

Dustin walked carefully down the center of the room, far from any exhibits. He knew there was nothing alive in here, but the darkness and moving shadows made things look alive. And what if someone really was here, waiting for them . . . ?

Brianne seemed to read his mind. "You know," she said, "something could be living here—something terrible—without anybody knowing, even Stone." She shivered. "Sort of like the Phantom of the Opera. You know?"

Dustin frowned. "Look. Don't let your imagination run away with you, okay?"

"Ha!" Brianne snorted. "Whose imagination is running away with whom?"

When they were almost out of the room, Dustin suddenly stopped. "Another one of the statues is missing," he whispered, pointing to an empty plinth. "But I can't remember which one."

"Me neither," admitted Brianne. She shivered. "This place is giving me a major case of the creeps. I'm *almost* scared enough to ask you to hold my hand."

"Me too," he admitted. He wished he could remember which statue was missing, but he couldn't.

Moving toward the main entrance, they hugged the corridor wall, holding their breath the whole way. Once in the main entryway, Dustin stopped beside the statue of the screaming boy. "Look at it. Doesn't this look like Tim?"

Brianne scrutinized the statue carefully, then shrugged. "It does look like him," she agreed. "But it looks almost as much like you. And I still don't know why anyone would want to hurt Tim."

"Me neither," Dustin admitted. "But I think we may soon find out."

"Where do we go next?"

Dustin thought for a moment. "I don't know. The last time we saw Tim and Brad was when Stone took them back his office."

"Oh, great," muttered Brianne. "We have to walk all the way back through the museum in the dark and then pay a visit to the professor?" She punched him on the arm. "Thanks a lot. If I die of fright, I'll come back to haunt you. That's a promise."

"Then I'm safe," Dustin answered. "You've never kept a promise in your life." He didn't like to admit that he was just as worried as she was.

He was a year older, after all, and he was supposed to take care of her. "If anything happens, I'll give you a chance to run for it."

"So you can tell everyone I was a chicken?" Brianne asked. "No way. I'm sticking it out."

Dustin was proud of her. Despite her fears, she wasn't going to wimp out on him. Still, they had to cross the museum again, and who knew what might be hiding in the shadows?

They moved carefully back the way they had come. Dustin strained to hear any unusual sounds. All he heard, though, was the gurgling of the heating system and the usual nighttime creaking of a building. He kept flicking his eyes around, hoping that if anything came at them, he'd see it in time to prepare for it. Still, the dark was so dense that an entire army could have been sharing the building with them and they'd never have known it.

People-shaped shadows wavered and moved, but he quickly told himself that his eyes were just playing tricks on him.

He hoped.

They had almost reached the corridor when Brianne suddenly grabbed his arm. Dustin jumped. "Don't do that!" he hissed.

"Listen," she replied, ignoring him. "Can you hear something?"

It was hard to hear anything over the pounding

in his ears, but Dustin concentrated. Finally he did hear scraping noises . . . not unlike the ones he had heard when the cat—or whatever it was—had been stalking the mouse.

"There's something out there," Brianne whispered. Dustin could hear the fear in her voice. "What is it?"

"I don't know," admitted Dustin. "Maybe that bird I saw in the tree outside, or that cat. Or maybe . . ." The cold worked its way deeper into his spine.

Brianne shuddered. "You mean that whatever is making those scratching noises could be anything? Thanks a lot. I really needed to hear that. I wasn't totally terrified yet."

"Just stay alert," Dustin suggested, sounding braver than he felt. "It'll probably be more scared of us than we are of it."

"I doubt that," Brianne muttered. Taking a deep breath, she nodded. "Okay, let's move out."

Dustin started down the corridor that led to the offices. The scratching sounded louder, and they held their breath. Then the noise faded, as if whatever was making it had taken off.

Dustin and Brianne continued down the corridor. As they walked, the hallway seemed to become darker and more menacing. The sharp shadows of boxes and cabinets loomed high above them, ready to reach down for them.

Then Dustin heard it again—the scraping of something moving in the corridor. At the bend, he waved for Brianne to wait while he peered around the corner. The hallway appeared empty at first, and he was about to signal her to join him when he caught a glimpse of something slithering along the wall.

He'd guessed about what was going on in the museum, but he wasn't prepared to see what he was seeing now. There was absolutely no way he could explain what was stalking the corridor.

He might have mistaken it for a cat if he had glanced at it quickly enough. It was about the size of one, with a long, sinuous body and tail. The face was catlike, although the eyes were a bit too large. The feet were a bit too big, too. It was the ticking of its claws on the marble floor that the two of them had been hearing.

But what made this thing so chilling was that it was quite clearly no mere cat.

Out of each shoulder grew a large wing. As the creature walked, the wings flexed and moved slightly. They were like bats' wings, tough and leathery, and each one was tipped with more claws. Whatever this thing was, it was a predator.

And nothing like it had ever existed before.

# CHAPTER 10

Dustin slowly pulled his head back around the corner. He put a finger to his lips to warn Brianne to be quiet. They both flattened themselves against the wall.

Dustin didn't know if the cat-thing would attack them, but he didn't want to find out. He could imagine its claws sinking into his skin. He jumped when something touched his fingers, but it was just Brianne. She gripped his hand ferociously.

Dustin understood. He felt better holding her hand, too.

The cat-thing then came fully into view. Brianne stiffened as it glanced almost directly at them.

Dustin and Brianne held their breath. Would the creature spot them? Could it smell them? Maybe it could hear their hearts beating. . . . Dustin's sounded horribly loud in his own ears.

Then, miraculously, the thing turned around and ticked its way back down the corridor. Dustin exhaled with a quiet *whoosh*. Sweat trickled down his back. For several seconds he'd been truly frightened. Now he tried to control the panic in the pit of his stomach.

After a few minutes he loosened Brianne's grip on his hand and slid up to the corner to peer after the creature. There was no sign of it. But for the first time he noticed another turn past Stone's office. Maybe the thing had gone that way.

"Okay," he whispered. "It's clear."

Brianne stayed close to him as they quietly made their way toward Stone's office. "What was that thing?" she asked, her voice shaking.

"I don't know," Dustin replied softly.

Brianne shuddered. "Where do you think it came from?"

"Just stay alert. *Very* alert."

They had reached Stone's office. The door was half open, and there was no light inside. Taking a deep breath, Dustin slipped into the room.

It was large—twenty feet long and ten feet wide. At the far end was a single window, with a heavy shade drawn. In front of the window was a desk, piled high with books and papers. The other walls were lined with bookcases, filled to overflowing.

The rest of the space was taken up with six trestle tables. On each was a variety of small statues and tools. This had to be where Stone cleaned and maintained museum pieces. A couple of the statues were ones Dustin had seen on display, but many were not familiar. Recent acquisitions, he supposed.

There was no sign of a large statue from the Egyptian room, though. Maybe it was too large for this room? Or did someone—or something—have other plans for it?

And where was Stone? Dustin wondered if they'd have to check each room before they found the professor. That could take hours, and they would certainly be found by that cat-thing long before then. They'd been lucky to avoid it once. He couldn't imagine dodging it forever.

His idea of sneaking into the museum and getting some sort of proof that something terrible was going on was starting to seem pretty dumb. They couldn't even find Stone, and now they had a bat-winged thing to worry about. Dustin had run out of ideas. He turned to Brianne. "I don't know what to do."

71

"You're asking me?" Brianne muttered. She glanced around the room, and grinned suddenly. "I bet I know." She pointed to one of the bookcases.

Dustin glanced at it. The cases were built into the walls and were all neatly lined up. The right-hand side of the one his sister pointed at stuck out about four inches. And along the bottom there was a line of light.

"I don't believe it," said Dustin. "A secret passage or room behind the bookcase?"

"That's my guess," Brianne agreed.

They went over and stood by the case. Dustin could see that the bookcase didn't quite touch the floor. And there was definitely light behind it. He gripped the edge of the case and tugged it gently as an experiment.

It swung easily toward him. It was on some kind of hinge. It must have been well oiled, because there wasn't a sound as it moved. Dustin tugged harder, until there was a gap between it and the next bookcase. Peering around the case, he grinned. There was a doorway with a light above it. A staircase led down from it.

"Sneaky," Brianne said quietly. "Someone covered up the doorway with a bookcase."

Dustin nodded and slipped between the cases. Brianne joined him. On the back of the bookcase was a handle, and Dustin pulled the case closed again. If the cat-thing checked Stone's office, Dustin didn't want it to see that anything had been altered.

They now stood at the top of a flight of stairs that led down to what must be the basement. The stairs twisted to the right at the bottom, so Dustin couldn't see anything directly below. But he could hear noises.

There were at least two people down there, talking. He couldn't make out any words, though, because there was a throbbing mechanical sound. It rose and fell with a regular pulse and sounded like a loud mechanical heartbeat.

"Are you going to stand here all day?" Brianne whispered in an irritated voice.

"You want to go first?" growled Dustin. She shook her head, which didn't surprise him. He sucked in a deep breath and took the first step. The next one wasn't quite as nerve-racking. Finally he got to a point where the staircase bent to the right. He peered around the corner. Then he halted, stunned.

He was staring out into a large room that was jammed with equipment and machinery. Computers lined one wall, humming and clicking as they worked on problems. On another wall was a power generator. It was producing the throbbing sound. There were racks of equipment on the third wall. The fourth one he couldn't see. But it was what stood in the center of the room that held him in awe.

They were two massive cages, like hamster or rabbit cages. Each was a cube of about seven feet. Connecting the two cages were bars wrapped in heavy electrical wires. A number of glowing neon tubes and some metal were haphazardly tacked onto the framework. The construction looked as if it had been hurriedly assembled. Thick power cables led from these bars to the generator on the far wall. Smaller cables connected the contraption to the computers.

But it wasn't the cages that gave Dustin the shakes. It was what was in them. The left-hand cage contained Brad Watson. He was crying and shaking the bars of the cage. It was hard to make out his words.

The cage on the right contained the statue that had been missing from the Egyptian room. It was the life-sized sculpture of Anubis, the jackal-headed god of the dead.

"Jeez," muttered Brianne, crouched behind Dustin and gripping his arm so hard it hurt him. "Stone's got his own private lab. But what's all this stuff *for?*"

Dustin was unable to think of anything to say. He had been right—something terrible was going

74

on here. But what was Stone going to do with Brad? There was no sign of plaster or anything that he might use to cover a body. Whatever Stone's plans were, Dustin had a terrible feeling that they were worse than anything he had imagined.

# CHAPTER
# 11

Stone stepped into view then. He'd been working near the wall that Dustin couldn't see. He
moved toward the cage, frowning and concentrat-
ing on a clipboard he held in one hand. He ticked
items off with a pen he held in the other. As he
approached the equipment hung on the framework, he looked over at Brad.

"Oh, be quiet," he snapped, clearly annoyed.
"It's hard to concentrate with all your blubbering.
You'll soon be silent forever."

"I'll behave!" howled Brad, tears streaming
down his face. "Please, I promise. I'll be real good
from now on. Cross my heart!"

"Shut up," Stone snapped. "I'm not interested
in your pleas or promises. You almost damaged

pieces of art that are worth much more than anything you'll ever produce in your lifetime."

"You're going to kill me!" wailed Brad.

Brianne smacked Dustin gently on the arm.
"Brad's getting on my nerves," she whispered.
"What a wuss. He's worse than you."

"Ssh." Dustin put his finger to his lips. Brianne
was right. Brad was a sniveling little coward. But
Dustin didn't want Stone to hear them. And he
didn't want to miss anything that Stone was saying. He knew they were gaining some vital
information.

"I'm not going to kill you," Stone snarled.
"Well, not quite, anyway."

"You're not going to kill me?" Brad sobbed in
relief and dropped to his knees. "Thank you,
thank you, thank you!"

"You're disgusting," the curator grumbled. "This
process won't kill you, but from your point of
view, what it *will* do isn't much better. It will
drain all of the life energy out of you, reducing
you to a shell of yourself—a statue. I hope you
make a good statue, because you make a pretty
miserable human being."

Dustin didn't want to believe what he was hearing. It was even more monstrous than he'd imagined. To drain the life energy from a person . . .
was it even possible? Could Stone really do it?

With a shudder, Dustin knew that Stone could

do that. It explained only too well what had happened to Tim.

Brad stared at Stone in horror. "You *are* going to kill me!" he howled again.

"Stop that!" snapped Stone. "I'm going to take your life energy. You won't be dead. You'll just be asleep forever." He stared at the boy critically. "If you turn out to be a beautiful statue, you might just bring pleasure into people's lives. I'm sure that all you do right now is make people thoroughly miserable."

"Please don't!" Brad begged. "Spare my life! I'll be good—I promise!"

"I told you, I don't care what you promise." Stone shook his head. "You're pitiful!" He turned to the statue of Anubis. "But look at this magnificent being," he added. "Do you want to know what I'll do with the life force I take from you?"

"No!" yelped Brad. "Don't take it. Please don't!"

"Life is wasted on you," Stone growled. "I shall take that wasted life force and use my machinery here to transfer it into the statue of Anubis. Your life force will give the gift of life to one who will certainly appreciate it more than you do, and make far better use of it."

"You can't do that!" Brad screamed.

Stone snorted. "You think I'm not able to? Ha! Pericles!"

The Greek guard stepped into Dustin's view. With fluid motions, he strode across to the curator. "Yes, sir?"

Stone gestured at the guard. "You see, little rat," he told Brad. "Pericles here was once a statue like Anubis. Then, yesterday, I caught another disgusting little boy like you. I took his life force and transferred it into Pericles here. Now that boy is a statue upstairs, and Pericles is alive."

Again Dustin shuddered with horror. Tim *was* the statue! He glanced at Brianne and saw the same shock and fear he was feeling.

Professor Stone was clearly brilliant ... and completely mad.

"No," sobbed Brad, tears streaming down his face. "Don't do it. You can't! It's not right!"

"Not right?" Stone stared at the boy as if in shock. "Come now, don't tell me that your life so far has been one of a saint. I saw you bullying that horrid little boy and his equally nasty sister. Was *that* right? I saw you crash into my precious display case. Was *that* right? Don't you dare tell *me* what's right! You've wasted your life thus far, so I shall put it to good use. The rest of you will become a work of art." He grinned nastily. "Who knows—maybe some little boy in the future will draw all over you. It would be poetic justice, wouldn't it?"

"I don't care!" Brad sniffed. "I'll be dead when you're done with me."

Stone sighed heavily. "You're as dim-witted as you are disgusting," he said. "You won't be dead. You'll be suspended."

"I don't think Dr. Frankenstein down there is playing with a full deck," muttered Brianne. She was shaking now.

"We have to call the police," Dustin whispered.

Brianne nodded. Quietly she started to back her way up the staircase, but just then there was a loud humming from the apparatus below, and she stopped.

Stone gave a happy cry. "It's ready! Pericles, man the power generator. I'll monitor the procedure from here." He glanced around. "Where is Grimalkin? If he's watching that stupid TV again, I shall be very annoyed with him. Oh, well." Stone shrugged. "He'll turn up, I suppose. Now . . . let the transfer begin!"

# CHAPTER 12

Spellbound, Dustin couldn't move. His throat went dry, and his heart almost pounded out of his chest. He was afraid he'd throw up, but still he couldn't take his eyes off the scene below. Beside him, Brianne was also unable to move.

Ignoring Brad's pitiful whining and begging, Stone moved to the apparatus between the two cages. He manipulated the dials and switches. The whine from the generator rose in pitch until the noise was painful. The lights in the room flickered with the extra power load.

Brad was on his knees. Stone paid him absolutely no attention. Dustin couldn't hear the boy's pleas over the terrible whine of the apparatus, but it was clear that Brad was still crying for mercy

He wasn't going to get it from Stone. The skeletal man didn't understand the concept. Dustin felt sorry for Brad, despite the number of times he had given Dustin a bloody nose and pushed him around. Brad's courage had completely left him. Faced with what Stone had threatened to do, though, anyone would have been scared out of his wits.

As Dustin watched, a surge of power passed through the bars between the cages. The neon tubes started to light up and pulse with power. Rings of light shot from one end of each tube to the other with a regular rhythm. Gold, pink, and green lights reflected around the room, giving the whole space an unearthly glow. Stone stepped away from the apparatus, grinning hideously as he observed the event.

The whine from the generators was too high for Dustin to hear now, but his jaw ached, and he realized that the noise was still there. The amount of power being used for the transfer must be incredible! Dustin couldn't help but admire the equipment even though he hated the purpose for which it was being used.

The pulsing lights in the tubes started to speed up until they were moving so fast they seemed to be one length of light that was running from Brad's cage to Anubis's.

Then there was a giant flash of light, and the

pulsing became a steady beam connecting the two cages. Brad, still on his knees, was staring upward. Atop his cage was a weblike arrangement of wires and devices that pointed down toward him. This suddenly began to glow with a deep crimson light. Brad's mouth was open, but Dustin could hear no sound coming out.

The device glowed brighter, and then a dazzlingly brilliant ray of light shot out, completely covering Brad. Dustin shielded his eyes. When the afterglow died down, Dustin saw that the apparatus on top of the cage was glowing gently.

Dustin gasped. Brad was still kneeling, his face turned upward, his mouth slightly open. All the color had been drained from him; he and his clothing were white. The only touches of color on his body were the reflections from the lights.

Brad Watson had become a statue.

Power continued to race through the bars toward the second cage. There was another device on top of the second cage that was similar to that on the first.

It began to glow with a greenish hue, brighter and brighter. The light played on the statue of Anubis below. Dustin held his breath as the power peaked, and there came another intense flash of blinding light. Dustin shielded his eyes this time to avoid being blinded. As the power levels fell, he stared at the statue.

The sandy brown color was gone. The statue was now bright with life. Its skin was tanned, and the loincloth around its waist was bright yellow, trimmed with blue. A golden bracelet around each wrist glittered in the pulsing lights.

But the face . . .

The body of the Anubis was that of a healthy young man, but the head was still that of a jackal. Doglike, with pointed ears, it had a large skull, showing there was a sizable brain inside. The whole head was covered with dark brown fur. It was a hideous combination—the young man's body with the canine head.

Then the mouth opened, and Anubis drew in a long, deep breath—his first. His mouth was huge, and his teeth were pointed and vicious-looking. There was a flash of pink tongue. Then his eyes suddenly blinked open. They were large and a deep, intense blue. Anubis blinked and then shivered.

"I—live," he said in a soft voice that carried throughout the room. There was authority and power in his voice.

"Yes!" Stone exclaimed happily, stepping forward. "You do indeed, Oh Great One. Thanks to me, you have been granted the gift of life."

Anubis stared down at Stone, his canine face unreadable. "You have done this for me?" he asked. "Why?"

**84**

"Because I have the ability," answered Stone, opening the door to the cage. "And I am a great admirer of yours. Besides, I wanted to see if the procedure would work on you. The last statue I brought to life was of a human." He gestured toward Pericles. "I wanted to see if the process would be successful on a more unusual character."

"I see," said Anubis carefully. He stepped from the cage and looked around the laboratory. "And are this man and I your only . . . experiments?"

"No, no," Stone said excitedly. "I've been working toward this for a long time. I brought a couple of smaller statues to life first. I worked on a catlike creature that I call Pyewacket. He's a wonderful mouser and an excellent guard. Then there's Grimalkin." He frowned. "Now, where the dickens *is* Grimalkin?"

"Here I am," said a gravelly voice, "—watching our guests!"

85

## CHAPTER 13

Dustin gave a yelp that was echoed immediately by Brianne. The new voice had come from just a few feet away. And it was a voice Dustin recognized.

Dustin spun around and saw that they were being watched by a creature that was perched on the stair railing, gazing hungrily down at them. It was the same creature that Dustin had seen in the tree just a few hours before.

Grimalkin wasn't quite as shocking as Anubis, perhaps, but it was incredibly repulsive up close. It was also horribly clear to Dustin that this creature was a live gargoyle. It sat on the rail, staring at them, its face twisted into a sneer. Its dark gray body—about two feet tall—was out of proportion, with long, gangling legs and arms. The hands were large, and each finger ended in a vicious-looking claw. The creature had large, batlike wings, which at that moment were folded across its back.

But Grimalkin's face was the worst sight of all. Large, protruding, buglike eyes glittered evilly, and pointed ears quivered slightly as it stared at them. A thick, bony ridge ran across the top of its skull. Its mouth was a long, sneering slit that looked almost like a beak. Two tiny nostrils quivered midway between that gash of a mouth and the cold, staring eyes.

When the mouth opened, no teeth showed. But a long, darting snake's tongue slipped out. "Children," it said in its thick, gravelly voice. "I *love* children. Can I have one of them? I'm *very* hungry."

Up to this point no one had moved. Stone was frozen, staring at his pet gargoyle and the two intruders on the stairs. Dustin and Brianne had been too shocked by what they had witnessed to move. With Grimalkin's threat, though, Dustin moved—and fast. "Run!" he yelled at Brianne. "We've got to get out of here!"

He didn't need to repeat himself. Brianne was already poised to head back up the stairs.

The gargoyle spread its wings and launched itself straight at her. Its mouth was open, and its tongue vibrated in anticipation. It was aiming

87

straight for her throat, and Dustin knew the horrible creature was planning to rip it out.

Without thinking, Dustin whipped his right hand around in a fist. He'd never been very good in sports—he missed pitched balls more often than he hit them. But in this case he knew he'd never get a chance at a second swing. He put every ounce of his will and strength behind his blow. He had to protect his sister.

He slammed his fist into the gargoyle's chest. Pain raced all the way up Dustin's arm from the force of the blow. But the gargoyle was slammed back against the wall.

It yelped and slid down toward the floor, stunned and shaking its ugly little head.

Brianne stared at it in amazement for about two seconds. Then she took off up the stairs as fast as she could, Dustin hot on her heels.

"Stop them!" he heard Stone shriek from below. "Get them! Kill them! Bring them to me alive! Oh, just do something!"

"What did you think I was trying to do?" Grimalkin grumbled loudly. "Test my emergency landing gear?"

Brianne and Dustin shoved open the bookcase doorway and plunged through the space. They didn't take the time to close it, but dashed into the corridor instead.

"The alley door," Dustin gasped as he ran. He

was shaking with fear. "They'll be here any second. We've got to get away!"

Brianne didn't waste her breath replying. Instead she raced for the door. Behind them, Dustin could hear footsteps coming up the hidden stairs. Anubis? The guard? Stone? All three? Brianne fumbled with the chain.

"We don't have time," Dustin said, running on past the door to the alley. "They'll catch us before we get it open."

"So what do we do?" gasped Brianne, running right behind him. "Just wait for them to get here? That gargoyle wants to *eat* us!"

Dustin shook his head. "We have to hide," he said. "Then maybe we can find another way out. A window or something."

"Then let's move faster!" Brianne snapped, and shot past Dustin toward the Egyptian room. Dustin followed her as fast as he could.

"There they go!" he heard Grimalkin yell. "It's suppertime!"

# CHAPTER
# 14

Dustin easily jumped over the chain at the end of the main corridor. His gym teacher would have been amazed. He grabbed Brianne's hand and dived to the left—as good a way as any. They landed behind a large marble column. Brianne crouched beside him, panting and trembling.

Where was the best place to hide? Dustin thought desperately. Should they split up, so that one of them could get free and go for help? Dustin didn't know. Their last trip through the dark museum had been scary enough. This was much worse because they knew exactly what was in store for them.

Not only did they have Grimalkin, Stone, Pericles, and Anubis behind them but somewhere ahead of them was that bat-winged cat. And who knew what else Stone had brought to life? Could other creatures be waiting in the shadows?

Brianne looked so scared—almost as scared as Dustin felt. He didn't think she'd agree to split up. And there was a little comfort in knowing he wasn't alone. Plus, if they separated, it would be harder for them to defend themselves. They'd better stay together.

He just couldn't let anything happen to his sister. After all, it was his fault she was in this mess.

"This way!" he heard Grimalkin screech behind them. "Move it, you slowpokes!"

Could the gargoyle see them, even in the dark? It *did* have big eyes. Maybe the monster had excellent night vision. What if it could see them, even when they couldn't see it?

Dustin wasn't going to wait to find out. He gestured to Brianne. Then they raced for the door into the next room, praying that Grimalkin wasn't looking in their direction.

Dustin and Brianne ran as fast as they could through the first couple of rooms. They needed to gain some distance before they looked for a place to hide. They soon found themselves in the room devoted to the Pacific island tribes. Even in the darkness Dustin could make out the shape of the large canoe that formed part of the display. Seated in the canoe were models of the people who had built and sailed it. Were they all statues? Or were they more than that now?

Trying to ignore his fears, Dustin concentrated on figuring out what to do. In the room there were lots of display cases, some large carved statues, and, best of all, a reproduction of a twelve-foot head from Easter Island.

"Behind the head," he gasped as he ran. "Take a breather. I've got an idea." Brianne followed his lead. As they slid into the space behind the huge carved head, Dustin held a finger to his lips to keep his sister from saying anything. They were both panting, but Dustin hoped their breathing would be back to normal before anyone caught up with them.

They had to try to take out the gargoyle first. Even if it couldn't see in the dark, it could fly. That made it the most dangerous. But how could they defeat it?

Dustin had an idea, but didn't know if he could make it work. In the darkness it was hard to see anything. But he had been to the museum so many times before that he knew the layout of most of the rooms by heart.

Close to his head, he knew, was a fire-safety area, with a sand bucket, a fire extinguisher, and a rolled-up hose in a glass case. Did he dare make a noise and smash the glass? The hose could come in really handy—if he could figure out how to work it. But he doubted that he could do that before the others reached them.

That left the bucket and fire extinguisher. Dustin peered through the gloom. Finally he made out their shapes beside the wall. He grabbed the heavy bucket and handed it to his sister. He motioned for her to turn it upside down. She obviously didn't understand why, but did it anyway, tipping out the sand as quietly as she could. Meanwhile Dustin unfastened the fire extinguisher and hauled that into their hiding place, too.

In the dim light of a nearby display case he examined it. It was the kind that had a handle you pulled up before pointing it at the fire. Clutching the extinguisher tightly, Dustin gave Brianne a reassuring grin. She couldn't manage to return one. She was frightened, and Dustin couldn't blame her. He was just as scared himself, but he didn't dare give in to his fear. If he did, they'd both be dead—or, at the very least, two statues. . . .

Then he heard the sound of flipping wings and some grunting noises that were obviously made by Grimalkin. "What's keeping you guys?" the gargoyle screeched. "Do I have to do *all* the work?"

Grimalkin was on his own right now. Perfect.

Dustin stepped out from behind the statue, trying to pretend he was actually feeling brave. In fact, he was shaking so badly he almost fell down.

"Here's one morsel!" yelled Grimalkin happily. He swooped down across the room, heading straight for Dustin.

After waiting as long as he dared, Dustin jerked up the handle of the extinguisher and pointed it at the gargoyle. A spray of thick foam slammed into the creature. It squawked unhappily as the foam pounded it from the air. Blinded and cursing, Grimalkin fell to the floor.

"The bucket!" gasped Dustin, continuing to spray the beast. Brianne caught on and slammed the bucket down over the gargoyle. Dustin handed her the extinguisher, which was still spraying. "If you see any of the others, hit them with this foam," he ordered. Then he grabbed hold of a stone carving. It weighed a ton, and Dustin strained to lift it. But he managed and set it down hard on top of the bucket. "That should hold him for a while," he said, grinning.

But his good humor was dashed a second later as the guard, Professor Stone, and Anubis hurried into the room. He and Brianne were in major league trouble . . . and he had no idea what to do next.

# CHAPTER
# 15

With a shout, Brianne suddenly jumped forward and raised the extinguisher. The jet of foam splashed across all three of their pursuers, but they just shielded their faces and gasped and sputtered. The extinguisher was a small one, and the pressure was dying down.

"The floor," Dustin whispered to his sister, pointing to a spot just in front of their pursuers.

Brianne caught on and sprayed the last of the foam over the polished wooden floor in front of the three. When the cylinder was empty, she threw it at them as hard as she could. Stone yelped as it hit his shin.

Dustin grabbed her hand and took off across the room toward the next hall. Behind them, he was pleased to hear the hunters yelp as their feet skidded out from under them on the slippery floor.

"Smart thinking," called Brianne. "Now what?"

His trick had bought them some time. But was it enough to get them out of the museum? And could they chance hiding a second time? Dustin doubted it. They had to try to get out.

"The alley door," he said. There was no better chance, he figured.

Brianne, for once in her life, didn't argue. Together they ran back to the corridor, through the Egyptian gallery, into the marble hallway, and along its length as fast as they could. At the alley door, Brianne fumbled with the chain, taking out the broken link so that it fell apart. Dustin pushed back the box of books.

They were going to make it!

With a squeal of fury, the bat-winged cat, Pyewacket, threw itself at him.

Dustin barely had time to raise a hand to protect his face before the creature slammed into him, its claws fully extended. If Dustin hadn't covered his face, the claws would have ripped out his eyes. As it was, they tore into his arm. The cat-thing was a bundle of hissing, snarling fury, and it raked at him again with its claws. Dustin could feel the cuts start to bleed. His left arm burned.

Brianne screamed and snatched up one of the

books from the box. She smacked the creature as hard as she could with it. Pyewacket yowled and reared back to slash at her as she swung out at it again. Despite the pain in his arm, Dustin tried to punch the thing. The creature was fast, though, and beat its wings furiously. It moved back far enough to get out of their way. Then it swooped down again, zeroing in on Brianne this time.

There was only one thing to do. Dustin threw himself to the floor, tackling his sister as he went. The razor-sharp claws of Pyewacket missed her face by inches as she fell over backward. Dustin hit the floor with a bone-jarring thump that took the wind out of him.

Before he could rise again, he heard the sound of pounding feet. Dazed, he struggled to get up— and found himself staring into the furry face of Anubis.

"A good chase," the jackal head said gravely. "But it is over now." Anubis clamped one huge hand around Dustin's uninjured arm. With the other, it hauled Brianne up from the floor.

Pyewacket had recovered and fluttered back toward them, its claws held ready to tear at them.

"No!" ordered Anubis sternly. "There is no further need. They are my captives."

For a second it seemed as though the bat-cat wouldn't listen to the jackal-headed man. Then

Anubis opened his doglike snout and growled, his teeth bared.

Wisely, Pyewacket didn't attack. Instead, it flew over their heads, landing on one of the cabinets. There it started to lick its paws, as if attacking anyone had been the farthest thing from its mind.

Dustin realized that he and his sister had lost the fight. They were trapped now. His left arm still burned from the scratches Pyewacket had given him. His right arm was held tightly in Anubis's viselike grip.

Stone and Pericles came pounding up behind them. Stone's skeletal face broke into a death's-head grin as he saw Anubis with his captives. "Excellent, excellent!" he gloated. "Two more additions to my little collection!"

"Let us go," Brianne begged. "We won't tell anyone." Dustin had to admire her ability to lie. If they got out of here, *he* would tell everyone they knew . . . although he wondered if anyone would believe him.

"I have no intention of letting you go," Stone replied. "But you're right—you won't tell anyone anything. Very shortly both of you will be unable to speak—ever again!"

# CHAPTER 16

Stone marched past them toward his office. "Bring them along," he ordered.

Pericles reached for Dustin, but Anubis shook his head and tightened his grip. "Walk," he advised Dustin and Brianne.

Dustin nodded miserably, and Brianne silently went along. Together the five of them walked back to Stone's office. The bookcase was still wide open, and Stone led the way down the stairs into the basement. Dustin and Brianne had no choice but to follow. Pericles brought up the rear.

As he stepped out onto the basement floor, Dustin shivered. The apparatus was barely humming now, because Stone had turned the power down after bringing Anubis to life. But Dustin had seen what it could do. He noticed that the wall closest to the stairs—the one he couldn't see from the stairway—held several large control panels, which Pericles must have operated earlier.

Stone crossed to the left-hand cage and opened the door. "He makes quite a nice statue," he remarked, examining the shell of Brad. "He looks as if he's praying. How sweet." He chuckled. "I'm sure that nobody who knows him would ever suspect that this praying statue is actually that loathsome little boy." He turned to the guard. "Take it out of there."

Pericles nodded and bent to lift Brad. His tremendous muscles strained, and Dustin realized that Brad didn't merely look like a statue—he also weighed as much as a statue. With a grunt, the guard lifted Brad and carried him to one side. With another grunt, he set the statue down on the floor.

Stone turned to glare at Dustin and Brianne. "So you two interfering little busybodies couldn't leave well enough alone, eh?" he snapped. "Well, I'm glad. Now I can use you to—"

"We weren't interfering!" Dustin yelled. "We were trying to find our friend Tim—the first boy you turned into a statue." He nodded at the Brad statue. "We were even going to try to help *him*."

"How noble of you," said Stone. "Well, all it's done is earned you the same fate." He jerked his head at the empty cage. "Toss the girl in there," he ordered.

"No!" cried Dustin, shocked. "You can't!"

"Shut up," Stone snapped. He glared up at Anubis. "Well, do it."

Anubis gave a slow nod and thrust Brianne toward the cage. Stumbling, she fell inside, and Stone snapped the door closed and fastened it.

"I take it you watched the last transformation," he said happily. "So I don't need to explain this whole process to you, do I?"

"It's wrong," Brianne said, her teeth chattering in fear. "How can you do this to people?"

"People?" Stone snorted. "Dirty, disobedient children," he said.

"You're evil," Brianne snarled.

"And you're nasty," he snorted. "Enjoy being so while you can. In a few minutes you won't be enjoying anything ever again."

Dustin was terrified for his sister, and he knew he'd be next. They had done nothing wrong, except in Stone's warped mind. They had only tried to help their friend. They didn't deserve the fate that was planned for them. No one did . . . not even the bullying Brad.

Then a glimmer of an idea came to Dustin. If he could just . . .

Licking his lips, Dustin said, "This machine of yours is incredible."

Stone blinked at him, puzzled. "Yes, it is," he agreed proudly. "But don't think you can flatter me into letting you go. That won't work."

"No, I wasn't trying to," Dustin said honestly. He knew that flattery alone wouldn't work. "I just wondered how perfect the things are that it brings to life. I mean, look at Pyewacket—a cat with wings who can actually fly. That's incredible, isn't it?"

"Yes," agreed Stone. "My machine gives any creature I animate all the attributes of the statue. Take Anubis there," he went on. "He has a human body and a jackal's head. Now, that's something you don't find in nature! Only I could have caused such a creature to come to life."

"Really?" said Dustin, pretending to be impressed. "That's astounding! So what do you intend to use our lives to animate?"

Stone frowned. "I haven't given that much thought," he admitted. "I had only planned on a single transfer today. But I'll select something appropriate."

"You've got lots to choose from," Dustin said. "I'll bet you'll come up with something unique."

"Of course," said Stone. "I plan to bring to life the most fascinating collection of beings this world has ever known. Everyone will say I am a genius when I announce my discoveries. I am founding a world where anything that mankind can imagine can become real. Think of it—a world where unicorns can graze and satyrs can roam. Where *anything* is possible."

"And only you can make it happen," said Dustin. "Using the life force stolen from other, less-deserving creatures."

"Precisely." Stone rubbed his hands together with glee. "I'm so glad that you understand, my boy. You're making a valuable contribution to scientific discovery!" He turned to Pericles. "Come along. I'll need help to move the statues I select." He glared at Anubis. "You keep an eye on that pair. They're tricky."

"So am I," replied Anubis. "They will not escape me."

Stone nodded happily and dashed up the stairs. The Greek guard followed to do the heavy work.

Brianne had listened to Dustin silently. Now she glared at him. "Boy, some suck-up you are," she snapped, "acting as if it's an honor to be an experimental rat for that maniac."

Dustin was starting to feel a little hopeful. "Oh, I don't know," he said, trying to sound casual. "Does that mean you're going to start begging and crying for him to spare your life? You think that would work?"

Brianne snorted in disgust. "I'll never beg and grovel in front of him," she answered. "If I've got to die, I'll go with dignity."

Perfect! Dustin twisted in Anubis's grip and stared up at the jackal's face. He had to repress a shudder as he stared into those blue eyes. "So," he asked, "what do you think about all of this?"

Anubis bent his head and regarded Dustin. His eyes seemed to look through Dustin, into the center of him.

Dustin shivered under the awesome gaze.

"I do not understand your question," Anubis replied. As he spoke, his sharp teeth glittered in the light.

"Do you think what the professor is doing is right?" Dustin asked. He prayed that Stone had been correct in saying that all of the attributes of the statue had been brought to life in his process. That was the only chance he and his sister had of staying alive.

"Right?" echoed Anubis, puzzled.

Brianne laughed bitterly. "You're asking that monster for his opinion? Dustin, I take back every nice thing I said about you today. Your brains have turned to mush."

No, they haven't, thought Dustin. It was obvious that their strength couldn't get them out of here. And they'd tried trickery and failed. Now it was time to use their last weapon—their brains. "Anubis is the god of the dead," he explained. "He is the one who in the afterlife weighs the souls of the departed. He has to decide whether they have been good or evil, and then reward them for the way they've lived. Isn't that so?" he asked the jackal.

"Yes," Anubis agreed, turning his head slightly. "That is indeed my function."

"Then," Dustin said triumphantly, "I ask you to judge. Is Professor Stone right in what he is doing? He's taking living human beings and draining their life force to give life to things that were never meant to be alive. Is that right?"

Anubis stared at him uncertainly. "I . . . must consider the matter," he finally said. To Dustin's surprise, he released his grip on Dustin's arm. "Stay where you are," Anubis warned. "If you try to flee, I shall be forced to bring you back."

"I won't run," Dustin promised. "Not while my sister is in danger."

"Good." Anubis stood still, lost in his dark thoughts.

Dustin crossed to the cage that held Brianne. "How are you doing?" he asked quietly.

"Oh, wonderfully," she replied. "I'm thinking of spending my next summer vacation in here. How do you *think* I'm doing, jerkface? I'm ready to scream my head off." Then she sighed. "Still, you may have come through again." She glanced at Anubis. "You think he'll help us?"

"I don't know," Dustin admitted honestly. "He's supposed to be fair, but I have no idea what he'll consider when he makes this judgment. Maybe he hates kids. Who can say? But he's the only chance we've got."

"Wrong, pea-brain," snarled a familiar voice. Grimalkin flapped down the stairs and into the basement. The gargoyle was still dripping foam from the fire extinguisher. "You ran out of chances when you attacked me. Now I'm really steamed. I had to chew my way out of that bucket, and I need something to take the taste of metal out of my mouth. You'll do just fine!"

He launched himself straight at Dustin's throat.

# CHAPTER
# 17

Dustin couldn't back up, since he was right at the cage. He threw up his hand, hoping to shield his throat.

The attack never came.

Faster than Dustin could see, Anubis's hand shot out and grabbed the gargoyle in mid-leap. "No," he ordered closing his fist about Grimalkin's scrawny neck. "They are not to be harmed—yet."

*"Awk!"* The gargoyle squawked like a strangled parrot. "Hey, whose side are you on, anyway?"

"That remains to be seen," Anubis answered. He stared down at the creature he held. "But there is no need for your kind of violence."

"What a party pooper," complained Grimalkin.

"Okay. If I promise not to eat anyone, will you let me go?"

"Yes," the jackal-headed god replied. He opened his hand and the gargoyle fell heavily to the floor. "But I must ask you the same question that you asked me. Which side are *you* on?"

"Sides, schmides," grumbled the gargoyle, clambering to its feet and dusting itself off. "I'm on *my* side. And my *stomach's* side." He eyed Dustin hungrily and then sighed. "But I guess I'll just go into the corner right now and quietly starve to death. Don't mind me. Nobody ever does." He stalked off, muttering to himself.

Dustin was shaking. "Thank you," he said to Anubis.

The great jackal nodded his head. "You are welcome. But that does not mean I have chosen to help you," he explained. "If I allow Stone to proceed, he will need an intact specimen."

Dustin shivered. He hadn't persuaded Anubis to help them. Still, the jackal god was considering the idea and hadn't rejected it out of hand.

Which way would he decide?

Dustin felt Brianne's fingers through the bars of the cage, gripping his own good hand. "It was a terrific try," she said softly. "I want you to know that, whatever happens, I'm . . . well, I'm proud of you."

"And I'm proud of you, too," Dustin answered simply.

"Don't get all mushy on me," Brianne warned. "If I'm going to become a statue, I don't want to have tears on my cheeks." She managed a grin.

Dustin tried to smile but couldn't. The idea that Brianne might end up as a statue was too horrible to smile at.

Just then Stone came hurrying down the stairs, rubbing his hands together. "I've found the perfect thing," he said happily. "Oh, this is amazing, really amazing." He turned back and yelled, "Hurry up, you oaf! Get it down here!"

Grunting with effort, Pericles carried down the statue that Stone had selected. Dustin was astonished. It was a life-sized statue of an angel. The face was beautiful, and it had two graceful wings soaring behind it.

"Isn't that lovely?" Stone asked. He was almost dancing with excitement. "Imagine when *she* comes to life! A real angel, here on earth! Won't that be something?"

Pericles set the statue down on the floor with a thump.

Stone whirled on him furiously. "Careful with that, you clod! We don't want a damaged angel coming to life, do we?"

"It won't," Anubis said with certainty.

"Of course it will," snapped Stone. "You of all people should know that I can do it."

"You can," agreed Anubis. "But you shall not. I will not allow it."

Dustin felt a surge of excitement within him. "Yes!"

Bewildered, Stone blinked and glanced at the jackal-headed god. "What are you talking about?"

"I am the decider," explained Anubis. "It is my function to judge right from wrong, good from evil. I was reminded of my purpose by the boy, and I must be true to it. I have made my decision: this work of yours is wrong, and it must end."

Stone's face went purple with rage. "You—you *dare* to ask me to stop?" he squeaked furiously.

"I am not asking," Anubis answered. "I am *ordering.*" He turned his back on the curator and faced Pericles. "Bring down the statue of the first boy," he ordered. When the guard nervously turned to Stone, Anubis barked harshly, "Do it!"

"I'd do it if I were you," Grimalkin piped up. He was perched on a computer terminal, munching a mouse he'd just caught. "Anubis gets real mean if you annoy him." With a belch, he wrapped the mouse tail around his tongue. Then he swallowed it as if it were spaghetti.

Uncertainly, Pericles did as he'd been ordered. As he left, Anubis swung back to face Stone. "What you have done is wrong," he stated.

"How dare you judge me?" Stone yelped. "I gave you life."

"No," Anubis answered gravely. "You stole life from another to give to me. That is theft. You forcibly captured unwilling people. That is kidnapping. And you took their lives and left them for dead. That is murder. It is my function to judge, and I have made my decision. Your experiments are over." He crossed to the cage and unfastened the door. "Come out," he ordered Brianne.

"You bet!" she answered and shot out of the cage, crossing to join Dustin. "Now what?"

"Dessert?" Grimalkin asked hopefully, licking his lips.

"Now," said Anubis, facing Stone, "you will start up your machine. You have two more transfers to make. Then you are done."

"I will not take orders from you!" Stone replied angrily. "I made you. You must obey me!"

"I must be true to my nature," Anubis replied. "I am a judge, and I have judged you. You are guilty. You have stolen life from the innocent."

"Innocent?" Stone sputtered. "Vandals! Wretches!"

"Children," corrected Anubis. "They may not be perfect, but they still have to grow. You are grown and should know better."

Pericles clattered down the stairs, carrying the statue of Tim. Dustin felt excitement mounting.

111

"Into the cage with it," ordered Anubis. The guard did as he was told. The jackal-headed god then nodded. "And you must go into the other cage," he said.

"What?" Pericles looked worried. "What do you mean?"

"The life force that made you was stolen from that child," explained Anubis. "It must be returned."

Pericles paled. "You would steal it from me?"

"No," Anubis replied. "I ask you to give it back to its owner. You were created a thing of beauty—a statue. You were not meant to live. Be generous. Give the child back his life."

Dustin could see the struggle inside the Greek guard. He was a decent person, but he also clearly liked being alive. Would Anubis be able to convince him?

Finally Pericles nodded. "You are right," he agreed. "I cannot live if it means that this child is doomed. I will do as you request."

"It is good," Anubis said, smiling slightly.

The guard entered the left-hand cage and closed the door behind him. Then he stripped off his uniform and cast it aside. He now wore nothing but his loincloth and a proud smile. "I am an athlete," he stated. "And an athlete I shall be . . . forever." He struck the pose that Dustin remembered so well.

Anubis then turned to Stone. "Transfer them back," he ordered.

"No," said Stone. "You can't bluff me." He crossed his arms and glared at the god.

Anubis leaned forward and gazed into Stone's eyes. "I am the judge of life and death," he said softly. "Transfer them back—or I shall bite your head off." He roared suddenly and bared his teeth.

"You save all the good jobs for yourself," complained Grimalkin. "How come *I* don't get to bite off his head?"

Stone became as pale as a statue and fled to the controls. Dustin watched as he set them all, then crossed to the panels to throw the final switches. Anubis watched Stone very closely to make sure the man didn't try to trick him.

The process was the same as the one Dustin had previously witnessed, only without all the blubbering and screaming from the living victim. There was a flash of intense light in the left-hand cage. Then it faded to show that Pericles was a statue again. This was followed by an explosion of light in the right-hand cage. Dustin laughed with relief as the color returned to Tim and he blinked and flexed his fingers.

"I'm alive!" Tim explained happily.

"You sure are," agreed Dustin, opening the

113

cage door and grabbing his friend. "Come on out."

Tim did so. Then he stared in shock at Anubis. "What is *that?*"

"The person who saved you," Dustin replied. "I'll explain it later."

"Now," said Anubis, "the last transfer." He opened the left-hand cage door and removed the statue of Pericles. Then he stooped and picked up the statue of Brad. He positioned it inside the right-hand cage. As he turned, Dustin reached out to stop him.

"Thank you, Anubis," he said. "You've been very honorable and brave."

"I am what I am," Anubis answered, but there was a slight twitch of a smile on his lips.

"I'll miss you," Dustin said honestly. This last transfer would return Anubis to his frozen state and bring Brad back. It seemed a shame, really, considering what a louse Brad was and how decent Anubis had turned out to be.

"I don't think so," Anubis replied. *"I* am not going into the other cage."

# CHAPTER 18

"What?" Brianne looked puzzled. "But if you don't, how will we get Brad back? He may be a toad, but we can't leave him like *that.*"

"I do not intend to leave him like that," Anubis replied. "But I am the judge of good and evil, and my decision has been made."

Anubis turned to face Stone. "You have been found wanting. There is no spark of humanity within you. You have dishonored the gift of life that is yours. You will step into that cage."

"Me?" Stone howled. "You can't be serious!"

"I am serious—dead serious." Anubis glared at him. "You are not fit to live, so you will give your life to one who has time to learn to be decent."

"Never!" screamed Stone. He turned to flee,

but Anubis's hand shot out, grabbing the curator about his scrawny neck. Kicking and squawking, Stone was dragged to the cage and flung inside. Anubis then locked the cage and returned to the controls.

Begging, whining, and pleading alternated with threats and howls from Stone. Anubis ignored them all. He had carefully watched Stone run the machine the first time, Dustin realized. His hands operated the controls easily. There was a flash of light, and Stone's whining was cut off. Dustin saw that in the cage was the statue of a skinny birdlike man, his mouth open in a scream.

There was a second flash of light, and then Brad was real again, still blubbering and pleading.

"Oh, get a grip," snapped Brianne in disgust. "What a wuss."

Brad was still on his knees. He looked up, amazed. "I'm alive again!" he gasped.

"Yes," agreed Dustin, unfastening the cage. "And we all know what a jerk you are. Especially *him*." He pointed at Anubis.

Brad gave a gasp of shock and jumped back. Hiding behind Dustin, he shivered as he stared at Anubis. "Keep it away from me!" he yelped.

Brianne patted his arm comfortingly. "Don't worry, chicken-boy," she said smugly. "We'll look after you till you find your mommy."

Anubis glowered at the shaking Brad. "The gift

116

of life has been returned to you," he said ominously. "This time around, make better use of it. I am Anubis, judge of good and evil. If you misuse your life again, you will answer to *me!*" He bared his teeth and hissed at Brad. Dustin was astonished that Brad didn't faint dead away. Somehow he managed to stay on his shaking feet.

Anubis turned to face them all.

"I will destroy this machine," he announced. "You must leave here now and return to your families."

"Thank you again," said Dustin. "But what will you do? Where will you go?"

"I suspect that there is plenty of work for me in this world of yours," Anubis answered. "I am the judge of right and wrong, and much seems to be wrong here. There may be a need for my services." He smiled, which was not a pleasant sight. "Thank you for your help, human. And for reminding me of my purpose. Now . . . go."

"You don't need to tell me twice," Brianne said, grabbing hold of Dustin. "We're out of here. It's been a thrill—not!"

As they were leaving the basement, Dustin heard the gargoyle scratching himself.

"So," Grimalkin asked Anubis. "Got any dinner plans? I'm starving."

**117**

# Epilogue: The Midnight Society

*Dustin, Brianne, Tim, and Brad returned home. They never told anyone what had happened. As Dustin pointed out, who would have believed them?*

*Brad stopped being a bully. But he developed a nervous habit of looking over his shoulder all the time—as if he expected to see someone there.*

*Tim never again used his felt-tip pen on anything other than paper. He never played another practical joke on Dustin, either.*

*Brianne discovered that liking to read didn't make her brother a wimp. And she always remembered that Dustin had saved her life. But that didn't prevent her from teasing him . . . at least once in a while.*

*And Dustin? Well, let's just say that Dustin*

*showed a lot more self-confidence from then on. But he never visited that museum again.*

*As for Anubis, Pyewacket and Grimalkin ... well, as far as anyone knows, they're still out there somewhere. So I'd be careful if I were you. Someone may be watching your every move ... someone who'll judge if you're naughty or nice.*

*And I'm not talking about Santa Claus.*

*I hereby declare this meeting of the Midnight Society closed. Come back again anytime . . . if you dare. . . .*

# ABOUT THE AUTHOR

John Peel was born in Nottingham, England, home of Robin Hood. He moved to the United States in 1981 to get married and now lives on Long Island with his wife, Nan, and their wire-haired fox terrier, Dashiell. He has written more than forty books, including novels based on the top British science fiction TV series, *Doctor Who,* and the top American science fiction TV series, *Star Trek*. His novel, *Star Trek: The Next Generation: Here There Be Dragons*, is available from Pocket Books. He has also written several supernatural thrillers for young adults that are published by Archway Paperbacks—*Talons, Shattered, Poison*, and the forthcoming *Maniac*. He has written two stories in the *Star Trek: Deep Space Nine* series for young readers—*Prisoners of Peace* and *Field Trip*. John is working on his next book, *Are You Afraid of the Dark? The Tale of the Restless House,* to be published later this year.

# YOU COULD WIN A TRIP TO NICKELODEON STUDIOS!

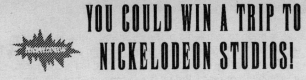 

**1 Grand Prize:** A weekend(4 day/3 night)trip to Nickelodeon
Studios in Orlando, FL
**3 First Prizes:** A Nickelodeon collection of ten videos
**25 Second Prizes:** A Clarissa board game
**50 Third Prizes:** One year subscription to Nickelodeon Magazine

Name_____Birthdate_____

Address_____

City_____State_____Zip_____

Daytime Phone_____

POCKET BOOKS/"Win a trip to Nickelodeon Studios" SWEEPSTAKES
Sweepstakes Sponsors Official Rules:

1. No Purchase Necessary. Enter by submitting the completed Official Entry
Form (no copies allowed) or by sending on a 3" x 5" card  your name and
address to the Pocket Books/Nickelodeon Sweepstakes, Advertising and
Promotion Department, 13th Floor, 1230 Avenue of the Americas, NY, NY
10020.  Entries must be received by 12/29/95. Not responsible for lost, late
or misdirected mail or for typographical errors in the entry form or rules.
Enter as often as you wish, but one entry per envelope. Winners will be
selected at random from all entries received in a drawing to be held on or
about 1/2/96.

2. Prizes: One Grand Prize: A weekend (four day/three night) trip for up to
four persons (the winning minor, one parent or legal guardian and two
guests) including round-trip coach airfare from the major U.S. airport nearest
the winner's residence, ground transportation or car rental, meals,  three
nights in a hotel (one room, occupancy for four) and a tour of Nickelodeon
Studios in Orlando, Florida (*approx. retail value $3500.00*), Three First
Prizes:  A Nickelodeon collection of ten videos (*approx. retail value $200.00
each*), Twenty-Five Second Prizes: A Clarissa board game (*approx. retail
value $15.00 each*), Fifty Third Prizes: One year subscription to

*Nickelodeon* magazine (*approx. retail value $18.00 each*).

3.  The sweepstakes is open to residents of the U.S. and Canada no older than fourteen as of 12/29/95. Proof of age required to claim prize. Prizes will be awarded to the winner's parent or legal guardian. Void in Puerto Rico and wherever else prohibited or restricted by law. Employees of Viacom International Inc., their suppliers, subsidiaries, affiliates, agencies, participating retailers, and their families living in the same household are not eligible.

4.  One prize per person or household. Prizes are not transferable and may not be substituted. All prizes will be awarded. The odds of winning a prize depend upon the number of entries received.

5.  If a winner is a Canadian resident, then he/she must correctly answer a skill-based question administered by mail. Any litigation respecting the conduct and awarding of a prize in this publicity contest may be submitted to the Regie des Loteries et Courses du Quebec.

6.  All federal, state and local taxes are the responsibility of the winners. Winners will be notified by mail. Winners may be required to execute and return an Affidavit of Eligibility and Release and all other legal documents which the sweepstakes sponsor may require (including a W-9 tax form) within 15 days of notification or an alternate winner will be selected.

7.  Winners grant Pocket Books and MTV Networks the right to use their names, likenesses, and entries for any advertising, promotion and publicity purposes without further compensation to or permission from the entrants, except where prohibited by law.

8.  Winners agree that Viacom International Inc., its parent, subsidiaries and affiliated companies, or any sponsors, as well as the employees of each of these, shall have no liability in connection with the collection, acceptance or use of the prizes awarded herein.

9.  By participating in this sweepstakes, entrants agree to be bound by these rules and the decisions of the judges and sweepstakes sponsors, which are final in all matters relating to the sweepstakes.

10.  For a list of major prize winners, (available after 1/2/96) send a stamped, self-addressed envelope to Prize Winners, Pocket Books/Nickelodeon Sweepstakes Advertising and Promotion Department, 13th Floor, 1230 Avenue of the Americas, NY, NY 10020

# Are You Afraid of the Dark?™

A brand new thriller series based on the hit
 show!

### #1: THE TALE OF THE
### SINISTER STATUES
#### by **John Peel**

### #2: THE TALE OF
### CUTTER'S TREASURE
#### by **David L. Seidman**

### #3: THE TALE OF
### THE RESTLESS HOUSE
#### by **John Peel**

### #4: THE TALE OF
### THE NIGHTLY NEIGHBORS
#### by **D.J. MacHale and Kathleen Derby**

### #5: THE TALE OF
### THE SECRET MIRROR
#### by **Brad and Barbara Strickland**

A new title every other month!!

A MINSTREL® BOOK
Published by Pocket Books          1053-05